MANDY

MANDY

by

Julie Edwards

Illustrated by Judith Gwyn Brown

SCHOLASTIC INC.
New York Toronto London Auckland Sydney
Mexico City New Delhi Hong Kong

ISBN 0-439-16254-8

12 11 10 9 8 7 6 5 4 3 2 1   9/9 0 1 2 3 4/0

Printed in the U.S.A.   40
First Scholastic printing, November 1999

for jenny
because i promised

Spring

The Discovery

1

ON THE OUTSKIRTS of a pretty country village called St. Martin's Green, there stands a large, white house called St. Martin's Orphanage. It has been there for many years. An imposing residence, the house has obviously known better days. It has generous, tall windows and large, high-ceilinged rooms. A black wrought-iron railing runs around the front and two sides of the property and the fourth side has a high stone wall to mark the boundary. The grounds, although not extensive, provide enough room at the back for a substantial play area for the children, a kitchen garden, and a modest orchard close to the high stone wall. The front garden is simply an expanse of green lawn and a drive extending from the gate at the road to the main entrance of the house.

The orphanage is managed by a board of trustees, but the principal figure, around which the institution revolves, is its matron, Mrs. Hannah Bridie. A graying, elderly woman, she is a widow who has been in charge of St. Martin's ever since the death of her husband some twenty years ago.

In her care she has, on the average, thirty children. Apart from ensuring that they receive as good an education as possible, she oversees the laundry, the food, and the cleaning of the home. She maintains discipline and tries to observe and help each child in a personal way. Her day begins at the first light of dawn, and she is never finished until late in the evening.

Most people would buckle under the strain of so much hard work, but this plain, good-natured woman seems unflagging in her energies, and although the home is constantly understaffed and she is underpaid, it is thanks to her devotion that the orphanage has a higher reputation than most other institutions of its kind.

Mandy had been there for as long as she could remember. She was a bright ten-year-old, with dark hair that fell boyishly straight and short, around her sweet face. Since she had no known relatives, the orphanage was her home, her whole world.

She had many friends and she was much loved. Because she had been at St. Martin's most of her young life, the staff favored her somewhat, and she was given certain privileges and more freedom than the other children. She could be trusted and relied upon. Apart from schooling and a few special duties, Mandy had plenty of time to herself.

Basically, she preferred to be alone. She was inventive and quick-witted, but, above all, she was a dreamer. Most of the time she lived in a make-believe world of her own. She loved to read. She exchanged books at the local library at least once a week. The wonders of *Robinson Crusoe* and *Alice in Wonderland* and *Gulliver's Travels* were very real to her and offered far more excitement than the reality of her life could ever provide.

On Saturday mornings she helped out at the local grocery store. She was given a small sum of money for her work, and she used it as she pleased. Most of her money was spent on her precious books and sometimes on paints, crayons, and paper for painting and drawing.

Only the younger children at the orphanage

attended school on the premises. Mandy, with the other older children, was sent out each day to attend the local school, which was on the other side of the village green.

Sometimes, after her classes were finished for the day, she wandered slowly home enjoying the pleasures of the soft countryside around her. She loved the outdoors and everything to do with nature. More often than not, having first obtained permission from the staff, she would go for a walk by herself.

She was rarely lonely at such times. The trees and flowers were very special to her and she knew the names of most of them by heart.

Living in her own dream world, as she did, it was never long before she had invented some situation to match her mood, and she was able to occupy herself for hours.

But it did not follow that Mandy was completely happy. How could she be? She had neither mother nor father and not even memories of them to sustain her.

She occasionally experienced very disturbing feelings. Sometimes she felt an ache inside that would not go away. It seemed then as though her life were very empty.

She would cry for no reason at all, seemingly, and it frightened her when she did. She tried to be brave and put away her feelings.

"I'm having one of my attacks again," she would think, trying hard not to let people see her tears.

Her attempts to keep busy were mostly an effort to fill her life so that she had no time to feel disconsolate. But the nagging sadness was persistent, and it would envelop her when she least expected it.

As Mandy grew, her longings grew stronger and sometimes she felt as though she must surely break apart with so much going on inside her. It was as though she were searching for something, though what or where it was she could not say.

2

THE HIGH stone wall at the back of the orphanage held a great fascination for Mandy. It was behind the orchard and stretched for miles to either side of it. None of the other children seemed to know or care what lay behind. But Mandy was immensely curious. She speculated for hours, wondering what lay on the other side. By standing on tiptoe she could glimpse many trees growing thick and strong.

"There's got to be something splendid over there," she told herself. "I just know there's a castle hidden among the trees. And I'll bet a handsome prince lives in it. He's probably very lonely."

Sometimes she imagined a forest full of animals that could actually speak to her. Her favorite dream was of a white unicorn that would follow her everywhere, who would lie beside her and put his head on her lap.

"I would call him Snow," she thought.

Her desire to see over the wall became an obsession. She felt that just a glimpse of the other side might reveal what she always seemed to be searching for.

She tentatively broached the subject to her friend, Ellie, a maid at the orphanage.

"Ellie, you know the big wall?"

"Mm-mm."

"What's on the other side?"

"Ooh, heavens, I don't rightly know. Just more country, I suppose."

"Has anyone from here ever seen it?"

"Not that I know."

One afternoon after school Mandy went to the wall and studied it carefully. At one end, a large apple tree growing on the other side thrust long, pink-and-white-blossomed branches over into the orchard.

Intrigued, Mandy went closer, and upon further examination, she found that a number of the big yellow stones in the wall protruded just far enough for her to gain a precarious foothold.

"I might just make it to the top," she thought. "With luck I could reach that big branch of the apple tree, and, once on it, I could really see for miles and miles."

The prospect of such a view was a challenge to Mandy's adventurous nature, and on an impulse she decided to try it that very second. She took a deep breath and began to climb. She hoped no one would see her.

9

Carefully, testing every stone before she put her weight on it, Mandy pulled herself up inch by inch.

At one point her fingers fumbled, and she clung for a moment, breathing hard. Then, with a last careful effort, she pulled herself to the top of the wall and threw her arms around the branch of the apple tree. Now, looking down, she found the effect quite frightening. The ground seemed a long way away.

"Wow, I didn't realize this was so high!" she thought. The orchard was awash with soft frothy blossoms. She turned and peered excitedly through the apple branches. An incredible vista was spread out before her, and Mandy drew in her breath with excitement.

She was looking at a whole new world: hundreds of trees stretching as far as the eye could see—most of them with that soft, silvery-green trunk and fine-textured bark that make the beech tree so easily recognizable. Sunlight filtered through the leaves in bright patches. The woods were open and clear—not dense at all. It looked wonderfully inviting and explorable. Mandy saw

a small footpath leading through the trees and longed to see where it led.

"I've come this far; now if I could just get down the other side," she thought.

She saw that the apple tree forked near its base, and it continued to subdivide, giving her numerous climbable branches. The bark felt smooth and soft beneath her hands as she eased herself to the ground.

"Now to look for my unicorn."

She set off along the path, which led into the heart of the woods. She was acutely aware of the blue sky, the heat from the sun, and the wonderful warm smell of earth and moss and flowers.

"Surely I'll find the prince's castle in a little while," she thought.

But each new dip and bend in the path revealed only more trees. She was just beginning to feel a keen sense of disappointment when the path suddenly widened, and, almost immediately, she found herself in an open and sunny clearing. It was quite wide, almost a grassy meadow, and dotted with evergreens.

Mandy could hear the sound of running water,

but her immediate attention was attracted to the far end of the clearing where stood a very old and very small cottage. Most of its windows were broken, and there was no door. Tiles had slipped off the roof, and the little chimney had a ridiculous tilt to it. It was in a very bad state of repair.

"Gosh, I wonder if someone lives here," thought Mandy. "Should I go and see? Ooh!—perhaps I'd better not." But her curiosity was stimulated. "It certainly looks empty. But there might be someone in there. An old tramp, or a witch, or an animal."

Matron Bridie was always reminding the children never to talk to strangers and to watch out for the unexpected, so Mandy quietly crept closer, keeping well out of sight behind the trees so that she wouldn't be detected.

She could tell that someone once must have cultivated a garden. There was a low fence, broken in several places, with a little gate. Underneath the weeds she could see the remains of a paved pathway leading to the space where the front door had been.

Mandy kept perfectly still, straining her ears

for the slightest noise. The gurgling sound of running water was nearer now, and birds sang in the trees. It was a perfectly lovely afternoon.

She moved closer and lifted the gate, which was hanging by a single hinge.

She tiptoed up the path, being careful to avoid a large patch of stinging nettles, and tentatively peeked through the doorway. She was looking into a small room. And it was empty. Mandy gave a big sigh of relief.

A staircase, seemingly, led to another room upstairs. In the back wall were two small doors. The house had no furniture. An old garden rake lay across the floor. Mandy moved to the stairs, treading carefully on the loose boards. Each step that she took caused little puffs of dust to rise and swirl in the shafts of sunshine that came through the windows. She climbed up into a tiny bedroom. There was no one about and no furniture here either. The windows were intact, but extremely dirty. Mandy wiped at the glass with her hand and had a splendid view of the meadow and the woods through which she had just traveled. A little brook was visible, too. It splashed and

danced along the base of a hillock and was enchantingly pretty.

Downstairs again and gaining courage with every step, she pushed gently at the first of the two small doors. It swung open, creaking on old hinges. She was in a tiny kitchen. There was a sink in one corner with a single, iron water tap attached to the wall above it. When she turned the tap, drops of rusty liquid dripped out and a spider scuttled from the drain.

There was a cupboard which contained nothing but a few broken bottles and an old tin basin. And there was a back door. Mandy pulled it open. She saw the remains of an old bonfire in the tall grass and a path leading around to the front of the house. Re-entering through the doorway, she went back to the main room and tried the second small door.

This one opened easily at her touch, and, as it swung wide, Mandy was totally unprepared for what she saw. To her amazement, she found herself staring at a room which was entirely decorated with seashells.

It was absolutely incredible. Lovely shells of

every shape and size and all colors of white and pink and iridescent mother-of-pearl lined every wall and the ceiling, too.

The effect was one of the most beautiful sights Mandy had ever seen.

The afternoon light shone softly through a big bay window at the end of the room. Cobwebs hung in silken strands. A pair of old curtains made of some soft material moved gently in the breeze coming through the open door. The woodwork and the window and door trimmings were painted gold, and the flooring was of tile or marble. A large fireplace was set into the wall, and the mantelpiece seemed to be of marble, too.

How this extraordinary room came to be in this small cottage, so many miles from anywhere, Mandy couldn't begin to imagine, and it was a full minute before she recovered from the surprise of finding it there at all.

She moved around touching the shells and the curtains, and looking into the fireplace. Everything was coated with dust.

She wandered outside to the clearing and sat down on the grass, drawing her knees up under her chin. She stared at the little house and garden for a very long time.

"Who could have lived here?" she wondered. "It can't have been a family, for there's just the one bedroom and the whole house is hardly big enough. Maybe somebody lived here alone. But what kind of a person would do that? And did he make the shell room?"

The discovery of this wonderful place was almost more exciting than finding a castle. The cottage was so charming and quaint. There was a quality about it—an entrancing air.

An idea began to take shape in her mind, and the more she thought about it, the more it appealed to her.

"What if . . ." said Mandy to herself, "what if I pretended this cottage were mine? I could sort of adopt it. Who would know? Who would care? Nobody lives here. I'm sure of that, now. And somebody needs to take care of it. And, oh, I *could* take care of it." She sprang to her feet. "I could. This place could really be mine, a house of my very own." She ran back into the little garden. "I could pull all the weeds out of here, and plant flowers and mend the fence and make the path tidy.

"I could sweep and dust inside and clean the shell room and wash the curtains and the windows. Oh—little house," and she turned to it. "I could take such *good* care of you."

Mandy went all through the cottage once more, seeing the rooms in a new perspective. A thousand thoughts ran through her head. She would have to make a list of all the things she would need. How was she to get them? And from where? She would have to be careful not to let anyone know of this secret place. It would be difficult to come here every day without being seen.

She had no idea how late it was getting until, suddenly, she realized the sky was darkening with the oncoming night.

"Heavens, I must get back. Matron will be worried about me."

Running across the meadow, Mandy paused briefly for a final look at her new-found delight. The little house was soft white in the gray dusk.

"I'll be back tomorrow," Mandy whispered to it, and, turning, she sped through the woods along the path she had followed earlier that afternoon.

She reached the high stone wall and swiftly climbed the old apple tree. Once onto the branch that extended over into the orchard, she eased herself down until she was hanging by her hands and then lightly dropped to the ground.

In a matter of moments she was inside the orphanage and racing up the stairs to her room to wash her face and hands before dinner.

3

MANDY SHARED a bedroom with one other girl. Her name was Sue. She and Mandy were close friends. The girls were almost the same age, Sue being the younger of the two by three months. She was not as strong a personality as Mandy and preferred to have Mandy take the initiative in all things. This suited Mandy very well and she happily allowed Sue to share most of her activities. There were times, of course, when this was not convenient, and Sue would sulk and feel out of sorts whenever Mandy expressed her desire to be alone. This was difficult for Mandy, for then she felt as if she were responsible for the other girl's happiness and well-being, and it lay very heavily on her.

But, luckily, these times were few and far between and generally the girls got on very well. They shared confidences and exchanged ideas. They even borrowed items of clothing and behaved much like two sisters would who were very close.

Being seniors, the girls were privileged to have a room to themselves. It was an attic bedroom, and Mandy loved it. She enjoyed being high up in the house, away from the other children. There was a small skylight in the roof just over her bed. Many nights she lay awake thinking and gazing at the distant stars in the sky above her. She found them very comforting, especially during the difficult nights when she felt troubled and disturbed.

But on the evening of the day she discovered the cottage, she was happily preoccupied with thoughts of the pretty little house and the wonderful afternoon she had had.

As Mandy and Sue were preparing for bed, Ellie, the maid, appeared around the door.

"Hey, Mandy, I found out something for you. You know you asked what was on the other side of the big wall?"

Mandy's heart skipped a beat. She busied herself and managed to appear nonchalant.

"Yes?"

"Well, Matron says it's a big estate in there. A really big one. Only nobody lives there any more."

"Oh, thank you, Ellie."

What a marvelous piece of luck. If nobody lived there, then she wouldn't be bothering a soul if she visited the cottage. It really could be hers. As she snuggled into bed and turned out the light, Mandy felt wonderfully content.

"Sue?" she whispered into the darkness.

"Mm-hmm?"

"Oh—nothing. Good night."

She decided that she would say nothing about the cottage just yet.

Mandy lay on her back, arms behind her head, staring at the night sky winking above her. She pictured the little house, alone and silent, under the same stars. Her mind was filled with plans and ideas and lists of things to get for it. It was midnight before she fell asleep.

4 ·᎒᎒᎒᎒᎒᎒᎒᎒᎒᎒᎒᎒᎒᎒·

THE NEXT DAY was bright and sunny. Mandy could hardly wait for school to be over. It was Friday, so she had only a half-day of studies, and all of the weekend before her.

Immediately after lunch, Mandy sped to her room and put on her oldest clothes. She ran into the garden and began looking for old Jake, the handyman and gardener at the orphanage. Mandy wanted to ask his advice and, possibly, borrow a few tools. She found him in the potting shed at the end of the kitchen garden. He was an old man, and very stooped. He wore exactly the same clothes day in and day out—black shiny pants, a collarless shirt with the sleeves rolled up to the elbow, and a dark-blue striped waistcoat. He brought his own lunch to the orphanage in a little tin box. His lunchtime drink was always two bottles of beer, and, predictably, he would snooze for a while in the early afternoon—propped up against the potting shed among the rakes and spades and brooms and buckets and pots of every shape and size. He knew just about all there was to know about nature. It was his religion and he spent most of his life outdoors, rain or shine.

He was just finishing his lunch when Mandy found him.

"Now, Mandy, don't you come bothering me. I'm going to take my snooze in a while."

"Oh, Jake, I won't stay long. I just wanted to ask you a few questions."

"Mm—Well?"

"Is it very difficult to weed a garden?" asked Mandy. "Do I have to know anything special?"

"Bless my soul," Jake looked surprised. "Whose garden are you going to weed?"

"Nobody's," said Mandy, "but is it very difficult?"

"Well, it depends on your soil." Jake took a

long drink from his beer bottle and wiped his lips with the back of his hand.

"You see, if it's good and rich and soft, then really most of your weeding can be done by just pulling at the roots, very gently, mind you, until they sort of ease out, and then you can shake 'em off and throw 'em away. But if the earth is packed and hard, then you need a small fork or trowel, and you sort of dig it in under the weeds, lift 'em up gently, and kind of shake the earth loose before pulling the plant out. But anyone can do it," he added, almost as an afterthought.

"I see," said Mandy. "Do you have a small fork I could borrow?"

"Thought you weren't going to be doing any of that," said Jake, squinting up at Mandy in a teasing way.

"I *sort* of am." Mandy didn't want to tell Jake about her secret plans. "It's . . . it's a project," she added hurriedly.

"Well, I can't let you take my things . . ." Jake began.

"Oh, I'll return it by tonight," Mandy broke

in. "I promise, Jake—just try me this once and see if I don't. By the time you get here tomorrow, it'll be back in the shed."

Jake wanted his afternoon sleep, and Mandy was in a persistent mood.

"All right, Mandy, but you're on your honor now. I hope you can be trusted." He slowly got up and found her a small fork. It was old and had a smooth, worn handle.

"Oh, Jake, thank you." Mandy beamed with delight.

"You just bring it back." He seemed rather pleased with himself. "Now, since you're borrowing that, what about a rake to smooth your garden over when the weeds are out?" he added.

Mandy could have hugged him.

Gathering up the tools, she hurried around to the back door of the orphanage. Leaving the rake and the fork on the doorstep, she burst into the big kitchen and found Alice, the cook, just sitting down at the large wooden table to eat her own belated lunch.

"Alice, could I please have some bread and

butter and water to take out for the afternoon?" She moved quickly behind the lady and threw her arms around her shoulders in a hug. "I'm going for a long walk, and I won't be back 'til dinner."

Alice had her mouth full, but she pointed at the pantry. "Bread's in there and a couple of scones, too. Help yourself. You can use one of those old ginger-beer bottles for water."

Mandy buttered the bread and the scones and rinsed out the bottle and filled it with fresh, cold water.

"You don't have any old dusters you don't want, do you?" she suddenly asked, and then, seeing the surprised look on the cook's face, she added, rather lamely, "I thought I might do my room later."

Alice smiled. She heaved her big frame up from the table and went to the cupboard under the sink. "Will this do?" She held up a torn piece of muslin about the size of a kitchen towel.

"O-o-o-h, yes," Mandy sighed happily. "Thank you, Alice."

She gathered up her food and her water and

her duster and slammed out of the kitchen door. Well-laden, she staggered into the orchard a few moments later.

The problem for Mandy was how to get all of her things over the wall. She finally decided to tie everything up in the muslin cloth and attach that to the big rake. Then she placed it in an upright position against the wall. Finding the same footholds she had used the previous day, she scrambled to the top.

Leaning down carefuly, she took hold of the rake and and eased it safely up beside her. Then she let it down on the other side of the wall and swung herself into the apple tree. Within seconds she was racing along the pathway, clutching her possessions, her whole being filled with anticipation and excitement at the thought of seeing the cottage once again. She burst through the trees into the clearing and stopped short. A fat rabbit disappeared quickly into the bank by the stream. A blackbird "tick-ticked" and flew into the trees. She was afraid she had dreamed it all yesterday, but there it was—solid and welcoming.

It was a glorious afternoon. The sun beat down and the scent of the earth mingled with grass and clover. Mandy noticed a May tree that she hadn't seen the day before. It was in full bloom. Behind the house there was a bank of rhododendrons, their fat buds due to open almost any day now.

There was so much she wanted to do and to see. It would obviously be impossible to do all that needed to be done this afternoon. Since Jake had lent her the rake and the fork, and she had promised to return them by the evening, and since the weather was so fine, she decided to attend to the garden first. The cottage could always be cleaned on a rainy day.

So she set her things down by the door and surveyed the garden. *Her* garden. The little path was obviously the first thing to be cleared. She decided to begin by the front doorstep.

Kneeling down, she pulled at the long weeds. To her delight they came out of the ground very easily. Carefully and methodically, she worked her way toward the little gate, avoiding the patch of stinging nettles. She made a mental note to try to get a pair of gardening gloves. They would really help to protect her hands on some of the rougher jobs.

She discovered pale gray flagstones beneath the weeds; so she cleared out all the grass around them and in between them.

It was a big improvement the minute the path was cleared. It gave her a real sense of what needed to be done next. The clean line of the flagstones directed her attention to a very pretty wild-rose tree that was growing around the door. It needed tying back. Mandy made another note to try to get some twine the following day.

Next to the door there were Michaelmas daisies—dry and dusty looking stalks, closely growing. They were not yet in bloom, but would be a fine splash of color by late summer.

There were many shrubs and flowers that Mandy didn't recognize, but she knew some of the wild flowers and left them in the ground. She wasn't sure what to do about the weed called convolvulus. It was growing over everything and although Mandy knew that it produced a pretty, white trumpetlike flower, she decided to pull it all out, feeling that its many tendrils might choke some of the better things.

She worked hard all afternoon. Her back began to ache and her knees were scraped and dirty. She became so warm in the full sun that she removed her cardigan. She was totally engrossed in her work. Every foot of earth that she cleared seemed to reveal some new treasure. She was fascinated by the beauty of the snails and the long worms that came to light. At one point she discovered an anthill and watched it with wonder. The little insects were so busy and seemed to have such a sense of purpose. Mandy wished she could be part of their world for just a little while. A sparrow came and perched on the low fence and watched her with a beady eye. Wood pigeons cooed softly in the trees, where they probably had a nest.

By late afternoon Mandy had cleared a path and one whole side of the garden. Near the fence she discovered quite a large clump of nasturtiums. They would soon be glorious colors of red, orange, yellow, and gold.

Mandy wiped her brow. She was hot and thirsty.

She decided to rest for a moment. Fetching her bread and scones and water, she sat on the front doorstep and contemplated her work. Now that the garden was partially cleared, it was easier to guess at its original shape and form. There must once have been a tiny lawn, and flower beds under the windows and along the fence. There was a box hedge running around the back of the house and a lot of privet hedges, too. They would need trimming and the grass would need cutting. She would have to be nice to Jake and, perhaps, he would lend her some more tools.

She munched on her bread and drank from the ginger-beer bottle. She was feeling pleased with herself. The little stream gurgled nearby, and the afternoon was lazy and quiet.

"This is all too wonderful. I could stay here forever," she thought. She leaned against the doorframe. "I wonder what I should tackle next? The other flower beds, I suppose, especially if I buy some seeds tomorrow. I'll want to plant them."

She thought of the shopping she should do. Money was going to be a problem. She had pocket money saved, and she received a little every Saturday for her work in the grocery store.

So, tomorrow she'd have enough money to make a start on flowers and things. She'd also need a pair of gloves and some twine for the roses. Jake could help her with that. She would need a lot of things for the inside of the cottage, too.

Mandy got up and wandered indoors. She immediately noticed the old rake lying on the floor, and her breath caught with pleasure.

Well, at least she had her own rake and didn't have to borrow that from Jake. But how was she to clean the windows? Where would she find a broom and enough dusters?

She went into the little kitchen and looked in the cupboard. She examined the old tin basin. As far as she could tell, it was intact.

"I can get water from the stream for washing up. I wish I had a little stove. It would be fun to make tea and things. I must make a grocery list. Phew! Housekeeping isn't easy. There's so much to remember."

In the shell room she crossed to the fireplace and looked at it carefully. On the side, there was a little trivet held by a bracket. When Mandy touched it, it swung over the fireplace.

It must have been used for cooking. So, she wouldn't need a stove. Now, if only the fireplace would work. She would collect some wood later and try it. She decided to add pencil and paper to her list so that she could write down all the things to do and not forget them.

It was getting late and time to leave for this day. Mandy wandered through the cottage feeling the pride of ownership. She stood at her front door looking down the newly weeded garden path. The freshly turned earth smelled wonderful. She wandered slowly to the little stream and bathed her face and hands in the clear water. It was pretty and shaded there with green ferns growing on the banks. The water was no more than a foot or so deep. The hill beyond was solid with trees. It would be fun to follow along the stream one day to see where it went.

She put the muslin duster in the kitchen cupboard along with the ginger-beer bottle. The tin basin went into the sink. She took the weeds she had pulled around to the back of the house and put them with the remains of the old bonfire. She would be making her own bonfire there soon if the rubbish kept building up at this rate.

It was time to go. Gathering up Jake's tools, she headed toward the meadow and home, pausing just long enough to adjust the little white gate. Pulling it straight and setting it up neatly alongside the fence, she noted with pride that the little garden was already beginning to have a trim, cared-for look.

5

ON SATURDAY morning, Mandy emptied her money box and counted her savings. She planned to spend them when she had finished work at the store.

Sue wanted to know what she was going to do.

"Oh, buy a few things."

"Can I come with you?"

"Well . . ." Mandy didn't know what to say.

"I'll be shopping right after work. It would be difficult for us to meet. Besides, I don't quite know what I'll buy."

It was true. Until she found out the price of some of the things she needed, she couldn't be sure just what she would purchase.

Sue looked hurt. Mandy felt bad.

"Tell you what," she said. "If I do buy something, I'll show it to you later. I probably won't get much though."

She ran off down the hallway, yelling at the top of her lungs as she went.

" 'Bye, Ellie, I'm just on my way to the store."

Mandy rounded a corner and ran full tilt into Matron Bridie.

"Gracious, Mandy, will you look where you're going!"

"Oops, sorry, Mrs. Bridie. I'm terribly sorry."

"My, you're in a hurry this morning," Matron smiled, "and could you, please, be a little more quiet. I think the entire household now knows that you're going to the store."

"Yes, Mrs. Bridie. Thank you, Mrs. Bridie." Mandy scurried away.

Walking into the village, she passed Jake riding to work on his bicycle. She waved to him and was glad that she had replaced his tools safely in the potting shed last night. Hopefully, he would let her borrow them again. She would really have to keep on the right side of Jake and show him that she could be responsible and conscientious. Her garden would never be right if she were not able to borrow from him some of the things she needed.

Mandy worked hard in the shop all morning. She was there from nine until one o'clock every Saturday, and she always enjoyed herself. She loved the smell of fresh bread and bacon and coffee and fruit and vegetables. Mr. and Mrs. Jennings, who owned the store, were very good to her. She was too young to serve at the counter and to handle the money, but she did a lot of fetching and carrying. She unpacked the new goods and stored them on the shelves and made herself generally useful. Sometimes in the middle of the morning, she was given a hot cup of tea and a biscuit. She was usually so busy that the time passed quickly.

Today, Mandy was particularly anxious for her work to be finished. She looked at some of the items on the shelves. Soups, chocolate drinks, canned milk, cookies. Wouldn't it be wonderful if she had enough money to buy them all!

She decided that she would see how much she had left over after she had purchased her seeds, and then perhaps she would splurge a little.

At one o'clock she raced out of the store and down the street to the garden supply shop, with her wages clutched in her hand and her savings jingling in her pocket.

To her dismay she discovered that the garden store had just closed for the lunch hour. She peered through the window and saw the proprietor, Mr. Simple, clearing away some things at the back. She tapped urgently on the glass, trying to attract his attention, but he seemed not to hear her. She moved to the door and shook it hard. He looked up and she waved, making frantic signs for him to let her in.

He hesitated and consulted his watch.

"Oh, please, Mr. Simple—*dear* Mr. Simple— do let me come in," breathed Mandy, and she pressed her face urgently against the glass. Wilfred Simple ambled slowly across the floor and unlocked the door.

"Well, Mandy?"

"Oh, thank you, Mr. Simple, I'm terribly sorry

to bother you at your lunch hour, but I need to buy some things—some seeds and things for a garden, and I wondered if you could possibly help me choose some. It's terribly important. I—I only have the rest of this weekend to do it in. It's a special project, and, well, could I please buy some now? I have my money."

He smiled at her.

"Come in. What sort of things do you need?"

"Oh, gosh, flowers, mostly. You know, packages of seeds that I can grow. Ooooh, what are these?" She crossed to a box packed with earth that was sprouting green leaf-clusters.

"They're pansies, ready for planting out."

"How much are they?"

"About four pence or five pence a plant."

"Five pence a *plant*? A single plant?" Mandy was aghast. "But I'll need so many. What about seeds? How much would they cost?"

"Well, it's a bit late for seeds, Mandy. You should have planted most of them in February if you wanted to have them ready for transplanting now."

"Oh, dear, what shall I do?" Mandy was in

despair. With everything so terribly expensive, she didn't see how it would be possible to fill her garden with all the lovely things she had in mind.

Mr. Simple put his hand on her shoulder.

"Now, it's not so bad. You don't have to buy pansies, you know. Come and see what else I have.

"Here, for instance. These are marigold seedlings and these are what you would call snapdragons, but they're really named antirrhinums. Now, they're not expensive. And these salvias would be lovely for your garden. They come up a gorgeous red, flamelike color and have a leaf that looks a bit like mint. They last a long time, too."

Mandy brightened. "Could you tell me how to plant them?"

"Yes, but first things first. Do you have things like a spade and a trowel and a fork?"

"Oh, I think Jake would lend me most of those things."

"That's good. Would he lend you a watering can?"

Mandy thought about it. "I don't think he'd

let me have it for that long. And I'd need to water almost every day, wouldn't I?"

Mr. Simple nodded. "Well then, let's see. What kind of a garden plot do you have?"

Mandy described it as best she could without saying too much for fear that Mr. Simple would discover what she was up to. He seemed satisfied, however, with the details that she gave him.

"All right now, here's what I suggest and you tell me if you like the idea. I think you need about thirty mixed plants. First of all, you should have some of these wallflowers." He got an empty flat-box and packed some wallflower seedlings into it.

"And marigolds would be a nice splash of color," he added them to the box, "and some of these salvias. Like I just said, they'd look lovely. This little plant here is called sweet alyssum. It smells marvelous in the summer. It's a little white flower, and it lasts and spreads all the time. It should go around the borders of your garden." As he was talking, he was packing more and more plants into the box. ". . . And I think maybe just a few big pansies would finish your garden off a real treat.

"Planting these out will be easy, Mandy. Just make a hole in the ground with your finger or a stick, place the seedling in gently, and make the earth around it firm. Put the plants a few inches apart. Then take this little watering can," and he took down a small plastic watering can from the shelf. "Now, see, it has a very good head on it, with the smallest holes, so that the water doesn't rush through and drown your plants. It lets out nice and easy, just like the soft rain. Water your flowers after planting, and they'll come up strong and healthy."

Mandy was thrilled. "Here," she said, putting all her money on the counter.

"Well now, the plants are a gift from me. The watering can doesn't cost very much." Mr. Simple picked up a few coins from the counter. "You keep the rest of the money, Mandy." He rang up the amount. "Is that all right?"

"Oh, Mr. Simple—" Mandy hardly knew what to say. "That's just marvelous," she beamed. "Oh, one more thing. How much do gardening gloves cost?" She had noticed some hanging on display.

"They're expensive. Why don't you ask Jake if he has an old pair he wouldn't need anymore?"

"I will," said Mandy.

She gathered up her box of seedlings and her watering can very carefully.

"Sure you can manage, now?" said Mr. Simple, letting her out.

"Oh, yes, and thank you very much."

"Let me know how they all turn out," Mr. Simple said. He smiled and watched Mandy walk down the road. Then he went back into his shop to his belated lunch.

6

MANDY HID her purchases in the orchard. The staff and children at the orphanage were at lunch, so she was unobserved. She took one look at the wall and her heart sank at the thought of getting the plants over to the other side. How was she going to manage it?

She was too late to eat in the dining room. So she went to the kitchen and ate a sandwich and watched Alice go through the piles of dishes.

She noted that Alice got a new package of soap flakes from the store cupboard. She wondered if she could persuade her to give her a package for the cottage. But—one thing at a time.

"Alice, I need a broom."

"Oh you do, do you? Since when did you decide to be such a housewife? Yesterday it was dusters; today it's a broom."

"I'd like some more dusters, too."

Alice laughed. "Now, what are you up to, Mandy?"

"Oh, just a game."

"Ellie might have a broom. I can give you some more muslin."

"Super." Mandy smiled.

Tomorrow, she would talk to Ellie. Meanwhile, Alice seemed in a good mood. She decided to see just how far she could go.

"Do you have an old saucepan or jug you won't be using?"

Alice stopped her washing up. She gave Mandy a long, hard look. "I might have. I'm busy right now. Ask me later."

"And could I take a box of soap flakes, please?"

Alice shook her head. "No, Mandy, I'm sorry, but these things cost money, and Matron wouldn't want me to be giving things like that away. Now, I've already said I'll see if I can find a pan or something, and you'll get your dusters, but that's enough."

"All right." Mandy decided to change the subject. "I'd like to take some bread and butter again today. I'm going to be out most of the afternoon."

Alice laughed. "You're a fine one. All this talk about cleaning up and the next thing you're going out. I don't know what you're up to, Mandy. You take care and be sure to be in by dinner time."

Mandy promised that she would. She fetched her tea and ran into the garden looking for Jake. She found him about to cut the edges of the front lawn.

46

"Hello, Mandy. You brought the rake back. I'm very pleased."

"I was wondering, Jake, could I please borrow the fork again—just today? I don't need the rake, just the fork. I didn't quite finish yesterday."

"I don't see why not. How's the project coming along?"

"Fine." Mandy smiled at him. "But, Jake, I need a few extra things."

"Oh. Like what?"

"Well, I need twine, and I really need some gloves so that the stinging nettles don't get my hands."

Jake stood up and looked at her thoughtfully. "This seems a very big thing you're doing. What is it, Mandy? Where is it?"

Mandy felt a rush of impatience. It was so maddening to have everybody asking her questions. She wished she didn't need to let anyone know that she was doing anything.

"I don't want to talk about it yet," she murmured.

"Wherever it is, it is not around here," Jake said emphatically. "We don't have a stinging nettle on the property. You'd better take care, my girl. Come on, I'll find you some twine."

Mandy trotted along beside him. He went into the potting shed and took down a ball of twine from a shelf.

"About this much?" He held out a long piece. Mandy nodded.

"I'll cut it up into different lengths for you. And gloves—gloves. Let me see now." Jake scratched his head and looked around.

Mandy's attention was caught by a large coil of rope hanging on a nail. If she could borrow it she could use it to tie around her box of seedlings and pull them over the wall.

"Try these on," Jake was saying. "They'll be big, but I think they'll do."

Mandy held out her hand, and Jake slipped on a glove which was at least two sizes too large.

"For what you need 'em for, they'll do just fine. Here's your fork and the twine. Now off you go. And be sure to bring it back by tonight."

Mandy dared not ask for another thing. She ran to the orchard and hid her things along with the seedlings and the watering can she had placed

there earlier. But, making sure that she was unobserved, she made her way back to the potting
shed in time to see Jake going toward the front
lawn. He did not see her.

She slipped into the shed and took down the
rope. After making sure the coast was still clear,
she raced as quickly as she could back to the
orchard.

She would have to be quick. Jake could return
at any moment, and some of the orphanage children might come along. She could hear their
voices as they played by the kitchen garden.

She took hold of the fork, stood back, and
hurled it as hard as she could over the wall. She
heard it land with a clatter.

Next she took up the watering can and threw
that, too. Because it was plastic, she didn't think
it would be damaged, just this once.

She tucked the twine and the gloves in her
blouse. Unfolding the long piece of rope, she tied
one end of it twice around the box of seedlings,
trying to tie the knot in the very corner. Then,
taking careful aim, she threw the other end at the
overhanging branch of the apple tree. After a

couple of attempts, it went over and swung loosely.

There was no one in sight. Mandy scrambled as quickly as she could to the top of the wall. She was in such a hurry and so anxious not to be seen that she scraped her knees and her hands.

Very gently, she took hold of the rope and drew the box up toward her. It swayed and bumped against the wall and, for one heart-stopping moment, Mandy felt she would lose all her plants. Some of the packed earth spilled to the ground.

She held the rope steady and gradually the swaying stopped. Beads of perspiration stood out on her forehead. She hoped no one would see her. There was nowhere she could hide herself and she was absolutely committed now to getting the box over the wall.

It was within reach. Holding the apple-tree branch with one hand, Mandy reached down and grabbed the rope firmly where it knotted at the center. She pulled it to the top of the wall and slowly let it down the other side, playing out the rope inch by inch. She felt the box touch the ground gently, and she heaved a sigh of relief.

She was down the apple tree and untying the knots in a second. Her precious plants were safe.

Now, all she had to do was return the rope and gather up her food that she had left in the orchard. She found the fork and the watering can and put them beside the seedlings. She coiled the rope and slung it over her shoulder and climbed the apple tree once more. She was just about to put her leg over the top of the wall when she heard someone calling her name.

"Mandy!"

She hunched down and prayed that she hadn't been seen.

"M-a-n-d-y-y!"

The voice was nearer. Lifting her head carefully, she looked over the wall. It was Sue, wandering disconsolately through the orchard.

Mandy bit her lip in annoyance. Why did Sue have to come along right now? Why did she have to call at the very moment when time was so precious and she had so much to get done? She huddled into the tree and kept very quiet.

Sue came to a stop almost underneath the overhanging branch, and Mandy held her breath, feeling her head would burst. It would be so easy to respond to Sue's call. So simple to tell her about everything. But the cottage was her secret. She had found it. It *belonged* to her. She didn't want to share. Not just yet.

Sue gave a big sigh. Then she wandered off, disappearing through the orchard trees.

Mandy was over the wall in a second. Her legs were aching from crouching. She raced to the potting shed and hung the coil of rope back on the nail. Then sprinting back into the orchard, she took the little package containing her tea from its hiding place under a bush. She tucked it inside her blouse and climbed the big wall for the third time that day. She was absolutely exhausted by the time she reached the cottage, but she still had a full afternoon's work to do.

7

MANDY KNEW that she must get her plants bedded out by the end of the day or they would suffer. She looked upon them as her children. They were her responsibility. Only she could give them care and nourishment. Without her they would die.

She cleared the weeds from the other flower bed under the windows. She picked up the old rake from the floor inside the house and smoothed over the earth. With the work that she had done yesterday, she now had two completely cleared beds, and she decided that she had just enough plants to fill them.

It was with mixed feelings of anticipation and pride that she laid out her seedlings. First came the wallflowers, right under the windows against the wall. Next, she planted the salvias, and then the marigolds. She spaced the pansies in front, and last of all, as a border, she planted the sweet alyssum. She made many trips to the little stream to fill her watering can. After each trip, she gently emptied the contents in a fine spray over her beloved plants.

When she had finished she stood back to admire the total effect. It was a trifle disappointing. For all her hard work and careful spacing, the flower beds still looked bare. The plants themselves looked bedraggled and skimpy.

She hoped they would brighten up by tomorrow.

She put on Jake's big gardening gloves and turned her attention to the stinging nettles in the pathway. After she pulled them out, the little paved area really looked neat and clean. She tied back the rose tree over the door. Every small thing she did made the garden look just that little bit better, which was very rewarding.

Mandy knew that she would have to return Jake's fork that evening. She was extremely weary and longed to sit and have her tea, but she decided to forego it and concentrate on the remaining two flower beds by the fence. If she could just get them cleared by tonight, she wouldn't need the fork anymore—not for a while anyway.

The sun was setting as she finished, and her aching knees and back told her that she would be stiff and sore in an hour or so. But it had been worth it. She was over the worst of the weeding.

She was so weary that it was all she could do to climb over the wall back to the orphanage.

She was not only trembling from fatigue, but working in the hot sunlight had given her a slightly dizzy feeling.

She couldn't wait to get to bed. At dinner she ate very little, and afterward she headed straight for her room.

Sue was quiet as both girls prepared for bed. Then she suddenly said, "I looked for you today, but I couldn't find you."

Mandy was brushing her teeth and was glad that she could use that as an excuse not to talk.

"U-m-m-m," she mumbled.

"I wanted to know if you bought anything today. I thought you might be by the big wall where you usually go, so I went there to look for you."

Mandy felt a kind of pain inside. She knew she would have to lie. And it was unpleasant. She hated fibbing to anybody.

"No, I went for a walk this afternoon."

"Did you buy anything?"

Mandy decided on a half-truth. "I bought some flowers from Mr. Simple."

She saw the surprised look on Sue's face.

"I just felt like it," she added and then, "but I

gave them to Mrs. Rose. You know, the old lady who lives in the cottage just before the shops."

Sue accepted this explanation. Both girls climbed into bed and turned out the lights. They lay in the darkness, listening to the sounds of bedtime all over the big house—slamming doors, children arguing or playing, the voices of the adults, firm and strong, establishing order, then quiet.

Sue spoke in a soft voice. "Mandy, shall we go to the old quarry tomorrow and play? It's Sunday and it would be fun."

But she got no reply. Mandy had already fallen fast asleep.

8

MANDY WOKE late the following morning. The children were clattering downstairs to breakfast when she finally opened her eyes.

"My gosh, it's late." Mandy sprang out of bed and then winced. Her back was stiff and sore from

56

all the hard work yesterday. She ran to the window and looked at the sky. It was a little gray and overcast, but she didn't think it would rain. She hurriedly brushed her teeth and washed her face and raced downstairs to the dining room.

"You're late, Mandy."

"Mandy over-sle-ept," chanted someone. "You'll be late for church, Mandy."

Mandy grinned good-naturedly.

Sue had saved a place for her at one of the long tables. She sat down and ate her porridge and toast hungrily.

"What do you want to do today?" Sue asked.

Mandy felt again that flash of annoyance that she had experienced yesterday. If only Sue wouldn't rely on her so much.

"I'm going to be busy," she replied.

"Doing what?"

"Oh . . . things."

Mandy looked at the spoons and the knives on the table. She wondered if she dared take one for her cottage. Perhaps she could get a cup and a plate, too. If she were careful she might be able to take something each day.

57

The children were made to clear away their plates after each meal. They carried their dishes and cutlery to the end of the room where they were stacked, ready for the kitchen.

"Here, I'll take these today." Mandy leaned across and picked up Sue's dishes. Before the other girl could protest, Mandy had put them with her own and carried them to the sideboard.

She made a great pretense of stacking the plates neatly. At the same time she slid a knife into the sleeve of her blouse. By cupping her hand and bending her wrist, she prevented it from sliding out.

"You'll be late for church if you don't hurry," Sue said, as the children left the dining room.

Mandy nodded. She raced up the stairs to her bedroom and hid the knife in a drawer. Throwing a sweater around her shoulders, she rejoined Sue just as the children were forming a double line for the walk into the village.

Most Sundays, Mandy enjoyed going to church. The little chapel was on St. Martin's Green, the wide grassed area in the center of the village, and from which the village took its name.

Church was the one big social event of the week.

Mandy watched Matron Bridie, dressed in the starched clothes that she reserved especially for Sunday, saying good morning to all the local people. Jake was there. And old Mrs. Rose. She hoped she wouldn't have to stop and talk to her for fear Sue would question Mrs. Rose about the flowers Mandy had said she had given her.

Suddenly, Mandy saw Wilfred Simple and his wife walking directly toward her. She knew exactly what Mr. Simple was going to say. It would be a disaster if Sue or any of the orphanage children heard the conversation. Without pausing to think, Mandy broke from the line and ran to the couple, forcing them to stop a good twenty yards or so from Matron Bridie.

"Good morning, Mandy. How did you get on with the plants?"

"Oh, fine, just fine." Mandy smiled nervously. "Good morning, Mrs. Simple. But, Mr. Simple, er—please don't mention the plants at all, it's—uum—well, they're going to be a surprise, you see."

"A-a-ah," Mr. Simple nodded knowingly. "A surprise for Matron, is it?"

"Mandy." It was Matron's voice, stern and reproving. "Will you please get back into line, at *once.*"

"Yes, Mrs. Bridie. Sorry." Mandy scurried to rejoin the children. She threw an imploring glance at Mr. Simple as they walked into the church. He winked at her and tapped the side of his nose in a conspiratorial way.

Sue was inquisitive. "What was that all about?" she whispered.

"Oh, nothing much. I just wanted to say hello."

Matron Bridie turned to the girls. "*Will* you two be *quiet?*"

Mandy sat in the church pew feeling nervous and uncomfortable. She wished that the service would be over quickly so that she could get away. During prayers she asked especially that her garden would flourish and her plants grow strong and healthy.

The light shone through the stained-glass windows and Mandy looked at the saints and apostles and hoped that Father Mulligan would hurry and finish his sermon. Today he seemed to be droning on forever. She thought of her cottage and felt a surge of excitement within her.

"Do not collect for yourselves treasures on this earth." Father Mulligan's voice penetrated Mandy's thoughts.

Her eyes flew open wide.

Had Father Mulligan been speaking directly to her? Was he referring to the cottage? Or did he know that she had taken the knife at breakfast this morning? Another glance in his direction showed him to be gazing at the chapel ceiling, fingers intertwined, pondering the value of his own words.

"—And besides, I didn't exactly *steal* the knife," Mandy told herself. "I really only borrowed it for a while. When I earn enough money I can buy one of my own." And so she justified her actions and felt better.

She sang the hymns in a loud, clear voice. When the service came to an end, Mandy was first in line for the walk back to the orphanage. Once there she managed to evade Sue and the other children. Collecting the knife from the drawer, she raced through the garden and was over the wall in an instant.

9

MANDY FELT free at last and exhilarated. Sunday! A whole day to herself! No troubles. No worries for the time being. And her cottage was waiting. She stood on the edge of the clearing, quietly enjoying the pleasure of seeing it again. It was the first time she had seen it in the early morning.

The day smelled fresh and clean. The grass was wet underfoot as she crossed the clearing. A family of rabbits scuttled away into the bank by the stream. Mandy wished that they would get used to her presence.

She noted, happily, that her plants had taken hold well. They looked stronger this morning.

She began a few chores. She put the borrowed knife in the pantry. She picked up the weeds from the previous day and carried them to the bonfire.

Mandy would have liked to cut the grass somehow and trim the hedges. She noted again the nasturtiums growing wild, and, suddenly, she had an idea.

"I'll transplant them into the other flower beds by the fence. I know that they grow very rapidly and keep on spreading. With any luck, they'll be quite a show once summer is really here. And I won't need to buy extra plants."

Carefully, she prepared and raked the ground, and then gently lifted a few of the trailing leaves. She made sure to leave a lot of earth around the roots.

Mandy scooped a hole with her hands and pressed the nasturtiums into it. She then proceeded to do the same thing with the remaining plants until they were spread out all along the fence. She fetched her watering can and sprinkled the plants gently as Mr. Simple had told her to do.

She tidied the area where the nasturtiums had been and stood back to look at the whole garden. "Now, I suppose I'll have to wait for a few weeks until they all come into bloom," thought Mandy. "I do hope they'll be all right."

She went indoors to the shell room and gazed at it for a long time. It was such a beautiful room. A peaceful room. Mandy felt calm and untroubled as she lovingly fingered the pretty shells. They were very dusty. She decided she would begin cleaning her house that very afternoon after lunch.

Ellie was cooperative, at lunchtime, when Mandy tackled her about the broom.

"Of course you can borrow it," she said. "Just put it back when you're done."

Alice called to Mandy just as lunch was finished. "I have something for you." She produced a roll of muslin and a small, rather old saucepan. "Will these do?"

Mandy reached up and hugged her. "Oh, Alice, that's super. Thank you."

She raced back to the cottage, almost tripping over the broom in her haste and excitement.

It was a perfect afternoon for being indoors.

The gray skies had become even grayer and soon it started to rain.

Mandy swept the shell room out thoroughly. She lifted the brush and pulled down all the cobwebs and went over the window frames. She brushed the shells as best she could and then used one of her dusters to clean them a little more thoroughly.

She brushed through into the main room, up the staircase and down again, and into the kitchen. All the debris went out the back door.

A lot of dust had arisen and settled back onto the stair rail and the window ledges. Mandy ran to the stream and dipped a fresh piece of muslin into the water and wrung it out. She wiped the dusty areas once again. She cleaned the pantry shelves and then washed out her dusters and hung them over the edge of the sink to dry.

She was filthy by the time she had finished, but very well-pleased with herself.

It was getting dark and Mandy was amazed how the time had flown. She decided to wait for the rain to ease off a little, so she stood by

the window looking out at the dripping black trees.

It was nice to be snug and cozy inside with a roof over her head to protect her. It would be even nicer when she could collect some wood to get a fire going.

A little sparrow was trying to take a bath in a puddle that had formed in the center of one of the flagstones in the pathway. Mandy watched with delight as the tiny creature fluffed himself out and hunched himself down with much ruffling and shaking of his feathers.

"He's like a small engine when he gets going," she marveled. "I shall bring some bread tomorrow after school so that I can feed him. Maybe I'll even build a birdbath one day."

10

THE FOLLOWING week was a busy one. On Monday immediately after school, Mandy went to the shops, and, with some of the money she had left, she purchased a small dustpan and brush, a scrubbing brush, a box of matches, and some scouring powder. She delightedly stored them in the pantry at the cottage.

She wiped all the windows and scrubbed out her sink and her washing bowl. The curtains came down in the shell room and she folded them away until she would have time to wash them. She tried to trim the edges of the pocket-handkerchief lawn with the kitchen knife and did a fairly good job of it. She even pulled up great handfuls of the longer grass and got it looking a little shorter, though it really did need a good clipping.

It was difficult finding enough time to spend at the cottage. School occupied nearly all of the day, and there was homework to do in the evenings. Mandy found it hard to concentrate on either. She longed for the summer holidays to come, when she would have more freedom to do the many things she planned.

Every evening at the dinner table she hid away a spoon, or a fork, and even managed a cup and a plate one night. They were all duly taken and stored in the cottage.

By now, she was quick and adept at getting over the big wall. There was always the worrying possibility that somebody might catch her, but she developed a keen ear and a sure instinct as to when it was safe to try. Nevertheless, it was always a bother to climb it, especially when she was carrying things. She wished she could find a better way to get to the cottage.

Mandy collected firewood every chance that she had. Walking to the cottage each day, she picked up any log or small twig that might eventually help keep a fire going. She made a woodpile against the wall just outside the kitchen door.

Toward the end of the week she put a few twigs into the fireplace and lit them. It was a disaster. Clouds of smoke filled the room, covering the newly cleaned shells and windows with a fine layer of dust. Mandy coughed and spluttered and ran outside the cottage to catch her breath. Her eyes were streaming with tears. She waited until the smoke subsided, praying that the chimney wouldn't catch fire. Finally, she went back indoors and tentatively examined the fireplace. Perhaps there was a flue or something that she should have opened.

Getting on her hands and knees she peered up the chimney and groped about for a possible handle. She was instantly doused with a liberal amount of soot.

"Oh, gosh." Mandy brushed her clothes in disgust. "Matron's going to be *furious.*" She would have to bathe and change as quickly as possible. But for the moment she was more determined than ever to find out why the chimney smoked so badly.

There was no flue of any kind, so obviously the trouble came from another source.

Mandy went outside once more. One side of the cottage roof sloped down to the hill by the stream. It was an easy matter to climb the hill and make a small jump onto the roof. Unsteadily, Mandy made her way up toward the chimney, dislodging the loose tiles and sending them skittering down to crash on the grass below. She made it safely to the rooftop and immediately saw the cause of her smoking fireplace.

It was a bird's nest, perfectly formed and completely blocking the top of the chimney. It seemed like an old nest, and Mandy was glad. She wouldn't have had the heart to remove it if there were eggs in it. She lifted up the mass of twigs and straw and looked down into the chimney to make sure there was no other obstruction. There was none, and so now Mandy had a fireplace that finally worked and a room so covered with smoke that it needed cleaning all over again. But it didn't matter. It was part of the fun of putting her house in order.

That night Mandy bathed and put her dirty clothes in the linen basket. She congratulated herself on being smart enough to avoid any comment on her disheveled appearance.

It was a surprise, therefore, when Sue turned to her at bedtime and said in a shocked voice, "Pooh, Mandy, you smell like you've been in a bonfire."

"What do you mean?" Mandy was startled.

She sniffed the air and then pointed. "It's your hair. It's covered with bits of soot. Where have you been?" Mandy thought wildly for a moment, then realized that Sue had unwittingly supplied an answer.

"It was a bonfire," she said. "I was helping Jake today." Sue accepted the explanation.

"Well, you sure do smell," was all she said in reply.

Mandy suddenly saw the funny side of the situation. Long after the lights were out, she lay in bed giggling helplessly, stuffing the pillow into her mouth for fear she would give herself away.

11

AT THE END of the week, Matron Bridie sent for Mandy to come to her study. Mandy was nervous. What could Matron possibly want? She went with great trepidation and an instinct that something bad was about to happen.

Matron Bridie wasted no words.

"Mandy, I gather that you've been spending a great deal of time away from the orphanage. I'm told that you have a project that you're working on. Would you care to tell me about it?"

Mandy experienced a moment's sheer panic. The palms of her hands were wet and she began to tremble. How much did Matron know? Who could have told her? Jake or Ellie? Possibly Mr. Simple? Or Alice? She wished she had been more careful.

"You must understand that it is very worrying to have you going off for hours at a time without our knowledge," Matron was saying. "The orphanage is responsible for you, and anything could happen when you're away from us like that."

"Yes, ma'am," Mandy whispered.

"Would you like to tell me about it? Could I help in some way?" Matron obviously knew very little.

Mandy hesitated, wondering what to say. Her mind was in turmoil. She was sure to be stopped from visiting the cottage if she told the truth. Yet she hated to lie. And what if she did lie and then Matron found out about it? But better to lie than to be forbidden to go to her beloved cottage again. She heard herself saying, "Well, I—I *did* have a project going, but I've given it up now."

"Oh?" Matron seemed surprised.

"Yes, I found a spot when I was out walking one day and thought it would be fun to try to make it into a sort of place of my own. You know, a little garden and things. But it was just too much to do, so I stopped."

She felt simply awful standing there. Everything seemed rather fuzzy. She was afraid that she would faint.

"I see." Matron looked somewhat puzzled. "Well, please know that I don't like your going out alone. I'd rather you didn't."

"I always told Ellie when I'd be back."

"Yes, I know, Mandy. You're a very sensible girl, and I trust you completely. But you must understand my position."

"Oh, I do." Mandy's voice was high and overly sincere. "That's why I stopped, Matron. I knew you wouldn't like my being out like that."

"Good." Matron seemed relieved. There was a

moment's silence. Mandy was sure her heart could be heard, it was beating so loud.

"I think you were wise to stop your project," said Matron thoughtfully. "But I'm a little sorry, too. You see, I do understand your wanting to make a place you could call your own. You must long for it very much sometimes." She smiled kindly.

Mandy suddenly realized that she was about to cry, and she swallowed hard.

"Oh," she said in a small voice, "well—it doesn't matter."

"I was wondering," continued Matron in a bright voice, "if you would like me to ask Jake to put aside a small plot in the garden that you could work on. It could be your special place. It might be fun."

Mandy forced her eyes to stay open wide. "No, thank you, ma'am. I've sort of lost interest now."

Matron gave Mandy a long and penetrating look. Then she said quietly, "Very well, but let me know if you change your mind. Now, Mandy, that will be all."

Mandy went out of the room slowly. Her eyes were brimming with tears.

12

ONCE OUTSIDE, Mandy leaned against the wall and let the tears flow. She couldn't understand why she was crying. Perhaps she hadn't realized how much the little cottage meant to her. The thought of having to give it up was unbearable.

She would have to be terribly careful from now on. She was sure that Matron was only half-convinced that she had told the truth. And Mandy felt so bad about lying that she really ached inside.

She decided that she would try to make a reasonable-sounding excuse for every trip that she made to the cottage.

She could say that she was going to stay late at school one day, or that she was going into town to visit the grocery store. A visit to old Mrs. Rose would always be acceptable. The weekends were going to be the main problem. There was always the excuse of going for a short walk, but she didn't think she could use it too often.

The next Saturday she told everyone she would be working a little late at the Jennings' store. Actually, she finished at lunchtime as usual and set out almost immediately for the cottage.

With her morning's earnings, she had purchased a bottle of concentrated beef broth, some biscuits, raisins, a small package of tea, and a tiny box of soap flakes. Also, she had saved a doughnut from her mid-morning coffee break.

Once at the cottage, she discovered she was famished. She skillfully got a fire burning in the shell room. Then, fetching her saucepan, Mandy filled it with cool, clear water from the stream and set it to boil on the trivet. To her delight it didn't take very long, and soon she was sitting happily on her front doorstep, drinking hot beef broth out of a cup and munching on raisins and biscuits and her doughnut. Never had anything tasted so delicious.

It was a brisk, sunny day, and Mandy looked at her garden and her plants, which were almost full-grown. They would be blooming in a week or so and she could hardly wait.

"I wish I could live here always," she thought wistfully. A blue jay winged back and forth across the clearing. He was finding food for his family. The same sparrow that had been bathing in the puddle the other day flew onto the garden fence.

"Hello, my friend," said Mandy and she smiled as the little bird cocked his head onto one side looking at her with a beady eye. "Would you like some crumbs?" Very gently, she tossed some onto the pathway, and, although he flew away for a second, the bird immediately returned and cautiously looked at the food.

"It won't hurt you," Mandy spoke in a soft voice. "Come on now." She sat perfectly still and suddenly the cheeky sparrow darted down and picked up the morsels.

Mandy threw him the last piece of her doughnut and he took that, too.

"I think you'll soon get used to me," Mandy said. "Now what shall I call you? Chip would be a good name, I think. That's the sound you make sometimes. Yes. Chip is a nice name."

She went into her little kitchen. She took the tin basin out of the sink and the box of soap out of the cupboard and carried them down to the stream. She filled the basin with water and poured the soap flakes in and stirred them around. Then she fetched the shell-room curtains and put them into the suds and washed them thoroughly. She rinsed them in the stream and wrung them and flapped them in the air to get the main creases out.

Mandy looked about her for a place to put them to dry. There was no clothesline and nothing to make one with. She thought of using the remainder of the twine that Jake had given her, but she feared it wouldn't be strong enough. Finally, she laid them on top of the box hedge and weighted them down with stones so that they wouldn't blow away. She washed out her dirty dusters and laid them out to dry, too.

She tipped away her washing water and watched the remaining suds move slowly downstream.

The water rushed and tumbled along, making a soft, soothing sound. Mandy lay back on the grass and gazed at the clouds.

"What a super afternoon," she breathed and gave a big satisfied sigh.

Turning her head, Mandy could see the rhododendrons, behind the house, in full and beautiful bloom. The colors were breathtaking, maroon and pink and white. The sun beat down and the trees made dappled shadows. Before she knew it, Mandy had fallen fast asleep.

She could not see the little baby rabbit, fat and soft, that came out of the bank to stare at her curiously. She would have been delighted to know that he hopped quite close, ears twitching, alert and cautious, to obtain a better view of the girl asleep on the ground.

Mandy awoke with a start.

She sat up and rubbed her eyes, then she squinted up at the sky and tried to gauge the hour. It was almost dusk and time to return to the orphanage. How lucky it was that she had awakened.

She gathered her things together and stored them away neatly.

As she started out across the clearing a very

large brown, gray, and white bird flew low over the grass, right in front of her.

Mandy stopped in her tracks. She saw the big blunt head and an enormous wingspan, which she guessed to be two feet at least.

It was a barn owl.

The beautiful creature soared onto the limb of a tree and Mandy kept absolutely still, hoping it wouldn't see her. The bird looked around with great majesty, turning its head from side to side. Mandy knew that an owl cannot swivel its eyes as a human being can, and so it has to turn its whole head in order to see to left and to right.

She must have stood quietly for five minutes or more. Suddenly the creature, without seeming to move a feather, tipped forward off the bough and plummeted to the earth. Now the great wings beat in the tall grass and for a moment the rounded head came up to stare bleakly in her direction. Then, lifting up once more, the bird flew away into the trees, a small mouse dangling from its beak.

Mandy felt mixed emotions. She was painfully sorry for the little mouse, but was delighted to

81

see the beautiful bird. It was a thrill to see him hunting like that.

She began to walk on home. Perhaps the owl lived nearby. If he did, then there were probably some buildings in the vicinity, for Mandy knew that barn owls prefer to nest in an outhouse or a barn. It was strange though that she had never come across any other buildings in the area.

She reached the big wall and resignedly climbed over it, leaving her world of nature and all things lovely behind, and rejoined the usual existence of noise and turmoil and children. It had been a wonderful afternoon.

Summer

The Garden

1

It became obvious to Mandy after a while that Sue definitely had the sulks. She knew the cause of the trouble. She and Sue were usually very close, but since the discovery of the cottage, Mandy had seen less and less of her friend, and, at times, had been quite rude about wanting to be alone. It was a bad situation.

One evening Sue said bitterly, "You're *always* going out by yourself. We never do anything together anymore."

Mandy tried to placate her, but Sue mumbled, "I just know you're up to something. I'll find out one day. You'll see."

The trouble was that Mandy began to feel very impatient. At first she tried to tolerate the other girl's mood, but, as time went by, she felt herself getting angry and that didn't help matters at all. One day things really came to a head.

Mandy had planned to spend a quiet hour at the cottage. Her plants were budding now and showing spots of color. With summer approaching there was always something new in the garden, or the clearing.

Mandy thought she had been unobserved as she climbed the wall, but, just as she came down from the apple tree, she heard a scuffling noise from the other side. Before she could hide, to her absolute horror Sue appeared at the top of the wall and gazed down at her.

"Hello. What are you doing?" she asked. Sue was smiling triumphantly, and Mandy knew that she had been deliberately following her.

She felt sick with anger, and it was with an effort that she managed to keep her voice light.

"Oh, nothing. I'm just looking around."

She wasn't going to give Sue the satisfaction of seeing that she was in any way disturbed by her presence. If she could just act as though nothing bothered her, then maybe Sue would get bored and leave her alone.

"You're not supposed to be over there."

"I know," said Mandy. "But you do things you're not supposed to do sometimes. I'll come back over though."

She started to climb the tree, but Sue said, "No, I'll come down, too. It'll be fun."

"But you're not *supposed* to. You just said." Mandy had an edge to her voice. "We'll get into awful trouble." She tried to sound concerned, and indeed she was concerned, but for a different reason. If Sue came into the woods, she didn't know how she could stop her from exploring and discovering the cottage, too.

"Oh, phooey," Sue was saying. "It'll be an adventure." She climbed down the apple tree. "Hey, isn't it super over here!"

Mandy wanted to hit out and push Sue away. Never had she felt so angry. She considered climbing back over the wall to the orphanage and just leaving Sue alone. Maybe without her, Sue would give up any ideas she had of looking around. But what if she went off by herself and discovered the cottage anyway? It was better to stay and try to avert disaster.

"Let's explore," said Sue.

"No," Mandy said in a loud voice. "It might be dangerous."

"Well, I'm going to anyway." Sue started out.

"Oh, all right." Mandy pretended to give in. "But I'm going this way," she said firmly and turned to the left onto a small track instead of following the bigger path to the cottage. It was the only thing she could think of to do.

Sue stopped. "Why?" she asked.

"I don't know. It looks more exciting. And there could be people on the main path. This way we won't be discovered."

Mandy walked on, praying that Sue would follow her. After a moment's hesitation the other girl ran to catch up with her. Mandy found herself trembling with relief. She strode out briskly, tight-lipped and furious. She wanted to get as far away from the cottage as possible.

The track kept parallel with the big wall. Both girls were silent as they walked. Mandy knew that Sue sensed her mood. The other girl was sullen and had an almost defiant air. There was not much to say.

"Must you walk so fast?"

"I'm sorry. *You* wanted to explore," Mandy replied.

But she slowed down a little. Somehow she would have to check her anger. She didn't dare antagonize Sue too much.

The wood became less dense. It was obvious that the narrow path was getting wider. A few hundred yards father on, it was joined by two other paths coming in at right angles to theirs.

The really interesting fact was that all the paths led to a large wrought-iron gate which was set into the wall. Mandy was immediately interested. She wandered over to look at it and noted that the main road passed by just a few yards beyond. She saw a padlock on the gate and then her heart missed a beat. It wasn't locked.

"Sue, come and look at this." Mandy pushed the gate tentatively. It didn't move. She applied her weight to it, and it slowly swung wide.

"Golly." Sue was almost as interested as Mandy. "Be careful, Mandy. Don't go out until you're sure no one can see us."

The girls peeked out. Not a soul was around. They emerged and carefully swung the gate to a close behind them.

"But this is the road that leads back to the orphanage." Sue seemed surprised.

"I know," said Mandy.

She was delightedly aware of the fact. If the gate could remain unlocked, and she could see no reason why it couldn't, then this was exactly the new way to the cottage she had been hoping for. This would mean no more sneaking into the orchard when people weren't looking. No more fear of discovery. Now she could really leave the orphanage in full view of everyone, as though indeed she were going off on some errand. She could then sneak through the gate and double back to the cottage. Mandy smiled. Things were going to be much easier from now on.

"I wonder where those other paths lead to," Sue was saying. "Oh, Mandy, let's go there again one day and explore. It was fun."

"Perhaps," Mandy said.

It was too late now to get to the cottage, and, since she felt almost thankful to Sue for having unwittingly helped her, she linked arms with her friend and they spent the rest of the day together. For the first time in ages, they enjoyed themselves and the hostility of the recent past faded away. For the time being, at least.

2

BY THE FIRST of July all of Mandy's plants were in full bloom. The garden was a mass of color and she was beside herself with delight. It was a small miracle. She was kept busy with a lot of weeding, for not only the flowers thrived, but everything else as well. But it was worth it. The roses were blooming around the door. The nasturtiums were bursting all over the front flower beds, seeming to have no sense of direction and growing in a wonderfully untidy way, the curling stems hiding and twisting beneath the big leaves. Their flowers were mostly a bright orange or yellow with an occasional mahogany red bloom. And they had a coarse, tangy fragrance—an unforgettable scent.

The wallflowers were tall and dark and strong and a sort of brick-red or yellow color. The salvias were bushy and sharp crimson in flower. And the beautiful marigolds! Mandy liked them best of all. They looked as if they had actually caught hold of the sun and it had burnished them to a golden orange hue. They stood so rigidly proud, a wondrous mass of tiny petals laid thickly one on top of another.

In front of them the lovely pansies with their sweet faces and beautiful blotched markings were in all colors of red, apricot, deep yellow, blue, and velvety black. Mandy couldn't believe that such generous blooms could grow on such fine stalks.

The sweet alyssum grew in clumps to begin with. But it spread and spread as the summer wore on. It gave off a sweet, delicate perfume that was particularly noticeable in the late afternoon and early evenings.

Mandy's garden received many visitors. Bees, snails, ants and worms, the beautiful butterflies, and all manner of tiny creatures that she'd never seen before. The birds came, too. Blackbirds, thrushes, chaffinches, blue jays, even a tiny wren. Chip was a constant visitor now and seemed to bring all his relatives, as well as his own babies, to visit.

Mandy loved it all. She worked in her garden every chance that she had. She purchased a large pair of garden scissors from Mr. Simple and painstakingly used them to cut her tiny lawn. They were the best thing she could think of in order to level the grass. It took her ages and her hands were blistered, but she found it all worthwhile.

She purchased other items, too: cornflakes, powdered milk, a small loaf of bread, sugar, and a pot of Marmite. Every afternoon immediately after school was over, she made herself tea at the cottage and sat on her doorstep, drinking and enjoying the peace and quiet before commencing her chores.

One afternoon she made a pleasant discovery. She had been trying to tidy up some of the weeds at the back of the house near the kitchen door. Mandy noticed a large object lying half-hidden in the long grass. She picked it up and discovered it was a garden broom. The head of the broom was made of fine twigs bound together, and it would be splendid for tidying the pathway and the doorstep and even inside the house. Mandy was delighted with her find.

July progressed and the good weather continued. Mandy used the new route to the cottage every day and found that going through the little iron gate made the traveling much simpler, especially when she had things to carry. Sue occasionally suggested taking a walk in that area, but Mandy always found a reason to dissuade her.

The summer holidays were approaching. Mandy planned to clean the inside of her house from top to bottom. She wanted to do it once the school term was over, so that she could really take her time. She began collecting a supply of cleaning things, so that she would have the items at hand when she needed them.

Funds were short, of course. But now that she had taken what she wanted in the way of cutlery and china from the orphanage, she began to hide away small things like a bar of soap, or a washcloth, and one day she stole a large box of soap from the store cupboard.

Mandy's conscience troubled her, but she told

herself that as soon as she had saved up enough money she would replace the items and no one would ever know the difference.

Unfortunately, the difference was spotted almost immediately.

3

MATRON BRIDIE didn't wait to summon Mandy to her study. She bore down on her one day immediately after breakfast was over.

Mandy spun around as her name was called. Her stomach kicked in panic as Matron's ample figure approached, reminding the already guilty child of a ship advancing under full sail.

"Mandy."

"Yes, ma'am."

"Have you been taking things from the orphanage?"

A pause.

"What things, ma'am?"

"Cutlery, crockery, some dry goods. Have you?"

Another pause.

"No, ma'am."

"I want the truth, Mandy."

Mandy felt that she was suffocating. She tried to look at Matron, tried to smile, but a pulse was beating at the side of her mouth.

"Mandy, *something* is the matter with you these days. I don't know what it is, but I do wish that you would consider telling me about it." Matron swept past her, leaving Mandy in a frightful state of anxiety.

The following morning, Matron assembled the entire orphanage in the dining room. She spoke in a very stern voice.

"Somebody in this house, I don't know who, has been taking certain items, and I want it stopped. Immediately. I am giving her one week in which to return them. If they are put back by the end of this week, there will be no punishment and I will say no more about it. However . . ." Matron paused and looked at the children. Mandy wanted to yell at the top of her voice, "It was *me*; I took them." But she bit her lip and remained silent. ". . . if they are not returned, and I do find the culprit," Matron continued, "and I *assure* you that I will, then, I shall be very angry, indeed."

The children buzzed with excitement. Who could it be? Who could have done such a silly thing? And for what reason?

Mandy went to her room and lay on the bed. She felt sick and very unhappy. Did Matron know that she had taken the things? Did she address the entire orphanage just to make her feel bad? Mandy couldn't be sure. But she was sure of one thing. This terrible feeling inside her had to be stopped. She couldn't live with her conscience much longer. She had been lying about her activities for so long now that each day the strain seemed harder to bear. Now, to have the extra burden of guilt about the stolen goods was just too much. Mandy decided there was at least one thing she could do to make herself feel better. She could return the items she had taken, and as quickly as possible. She resolved to try to work overtime at the Jennings' store on Saturdays in order to buy her own cups and plates and knives and spoons.

And that is exactly what she did. By the end of the week Mandy had returned everything except the soap flakes which had already been used.

That Saturday, and the next, Mandy worked a full day and was able to make enough money to purchase a plastic cup and saucer and a plate, then a knife and fork and spoon. She had enough money left over for a good strong kitchen knife and a can opener.

She felt much better about it and wondered that she hadn't thought to work overtime before. It took hours away from her precious weekends, but it was a good way to make the extra money she needed.

Matron made no more mention of the stolen goods, and things seemed to return to normal.

4

THE SUMMER holidays arrived at last. The days blended into one long impression of sun and hazy skies, sweet-smelling grass and summer showers staining the brown earth black. For Mandy it was the happiest time she had ever known and her every waking moment seemed filled with birdsong and the ripple of the stream and the colors of her flowers.

She cleaned her cottage from top to bottom. She swept and dusted and scrubbed the front porch and the stairs. She washed the windows again and hung the clean curtains up in the shell room. She put shelf paper in the kitchen cupboard.

Also, she found a large wooden crate at the orphanage and managed to get it to the cottage. She covered it with the remaining shelf paper and it made a good table. She wished she had a chair to sit on. Since that was impossible, Mandy looked around for a large log, and she soon found one that made a very good seat. Not that she used it much. She usually preferred to sit on the front doorstep.

The rabbit family became used to her comings and goings and eventually took no notice of her at all. Quite often, when she was working in her garden, Mandy would stop and quietly watch one of them hop into the shadow of the hedge to play.

Chip was present almost every morning and seemed quite put out on the few occasions when she didn't bring him bread from the breakfast table.

There were days when Mandy didn't bother to work on the house or the garden at all. She lay on her tummy in the grass and discovered that, even though her garden might appear to be totally still, the more she waited and watched and im-mobilized herself, the more she became aware that her garden was alive and moving in a hundred different ways.

It was a wondrous thing to discover an ant carrying something twice as large as itself, or a beetle moving slowly over the blades of green to an unknown destination. She watched the bees gathering nectar from her flowers and the small spiders scuttling in all directions. At such times she forgot about her everyday world and was transported into the kingdom of all things small where a butterfly seems like an overwhelmingly beautiful giant creature; where the smallest twig is a tree, and a pebble a mountain.

Mandy was lying on the lawn one quiet afternoon. She had been daydreaming for so long that she was in a sleepy stupor. Suddenly, she was aware of a movement off to her right by the stream. There was the noise of a displaced stone falling into the water. For one paralyzing moment she feared that she had been discovered. A hundred thoughts raced through her mind. Who could it be? What should she say? Should she get up and run? Luckily, she had the good sense to remain where she was, and it was as well she did.

When she carefully raised her head a few seconds later, she was rewarded with a most wonderful and surprising sight. A young fallow deer had come down to the stream to drink. It was standing so near to Mandy that she could clearly see the brown spots on the fawn coloring and the small lump of a tail with the white patch around it.

She drew in her breath with excitement and the lovely creature raised its head and gazed at her, seeming not at all afraid. For the longest moment it stood there, the prominent ears twitching. Mandy marveled at the creature's exquisite beauty—the delicate face with the almond-shaped eyes and the soft wet muzzle.

"Oooh," Mandy breathed. "You are lovely. Where do you come from? What shall I call you? Oh, please don't leave," she whispered. But the deer began to pick its way back into the woods, carefully placing one shiny black hoof precisely after another on the long grass.

Mandy watched until it disappeared almost magically through a shaft of sunlight in the trees.

"I hope he comes to visit again. I *hope* he does," she murmured fervently. "I shall call him Snow."

That night she dreamed of the deer. Strangely, the animal was holding her. She cuddled close into the soft fur and touched and kissed it gently. In the morning her pillow was wet with tears.

5

MANDY WANTED to borrow some garden shears from Jake. She needed them to cut her box hedges and trim her lawn properly. But she couldn't think how to get the shears without letting Jake know what she really wanted them for. She couldn't tell even a half-truth because he would know immediately that she still had a "project," and she was sure that he would mention it to Matron. Then she'd be in trouble again.

She still had problems getting away to the cottage each day. Her excuses were getting more and more difficult to find. She longed for just one complete day to herself, a day that could be free from worries and guilt and conscience. It seemed unlikely that she'd ever get it.

Meanwhile, there was the problem of the shears. She chatted with Jake one day about the garden and his plants, and in a nonchalant way she got around to mentioning the tools he used.

"Jake, your hedges are so nice—all neat and tidy. How do you keep them like that?"

"I use my big shears. Now, Mandy, you've seen me use them."

"Oh, yes," Mandy feigned surprise. "Aren't they heavy?"

"Yup." Jake was not in a talkative mood.

"Could I manage them?" Mandy asked innocently.

"I wouldn't let you."

"Why not?" She was startled.

"Because they're sharp, and they're my best, and they're not for the likes of little girls like you."

"But I could hold them, couldn't I? I mean, if you wanted to let me try them I could manage them? Couldn't I?"

"You could . . ."

Mandy smiled.

"But I wouldn't," added Jake, after a pause. "So keep your thieving eyes off, young lady." He grinned at her.

And that was that!

Mandy wished very much that she hadn't

brought up the subject. Now she was really stumped. She couldn't think of a single way to get around the problem. She let it go for a while, and just sulked every time she looked at her untidy hedges and her ragged lawn. She couldn't face the agony of using the scissors again—too many blisters that way and too much time spent on the job. And, anyway, scissors would be no good on the box hedges. She was determined to get those shears somehow.

And very suddenly a way presented itself.

Every August, during the Bank Holiday weekend, Matron Bridie took all the orphanage children on a day-trip to the sea. It was always a wonderfully exciting time and tremendous fun. The children looked forward to it each year. A charabanc was hired especially for the event!

This year, however, for the first time in her young life, Mandy had absolutely no desire to go on the excursion. She was far too preoccupied and involved with the cottage. She suddenly realized that, if she could avoid the annual outing, she would have one entire day to herself, which was exactly what she had been yearning for. And perhaps she could "borrow" Jake's shears without his ever knowing that she had touched them.

6

ON THE MORNING of the excursion, Mandy went down to breakfast with a serious face. She pretended she wasn't hungry and hardly ate a thing.

Afterward she approached Matron Bridie timidly. "Matron, I'm afraid I don't feel too well."

"What?" Matron seemed distracted. She was trying to gather all the children together for the outing. They were very excited and the noise was deafening.

"I said I feel rather queasy. I'm a bit trembly. I'm afraid I might be sick."

"Oh, Mandy." It was a sound of exasperation. Matron gave Mandy a long, hard look. "Do you have a fever?"

"I don't think so. I'm not sure."

Matron put her hand on Mandy's brow.

"No, you're as cool as can be. You'll be all

right. A day at the sea is just what you need. The fresh air will do you good."

Mandy began to feel desperate.

"Oh, but . . . I honestly don't feel like a whole big day. Couldn't I just stay here and rest? I really do feel very odd."

She was by now so nervous and tense that she did indeed feel odd. It was easy to be convincing. Beads of perspiration stood out on her brow, and she swayed a little.

Matron hesitated.

"If I could just lie down for a while, I think I'd feel better. I could sunbathe in the garden later."

"Oh well, you'll have to stay here with Ellie. There's no one else around. It's really maddening that this should happen today."

The distracted woman moved off to find Ellie, and Mandy ran up to her room. She wanted to get away in case Matron suddenly changed her mind.

Though she felt guilty, Mandy was filled with a tremendous sense of relief. She so desperately needed a little peace and time to herself and she quite contentedly lay on the bed in no hurry to make a move. Today was a day to be savored.

She listened to the children noisily departing below. She heard the big bus start up and accelerate away down the road. Suddenly everything was quiet.

Mandy felt that even if she didn't go to the cottage today she was still justified in wanting to stay home. The quiet alone was worth it.

Ellie came in to see how she was.

"Are you feeling a little better?"

"Oh, yes," Mandy smiled. "Really, I just was feeling a bit wobbly and sick. I'm much stronger already."

"Did you eat any breakfast?"

"No."

"Well, you know it could be that you're hungry. Would you like me to get something for you?"

"Oh, Ellie." Mandy was starving. "I think it would be lovely. Shall I come down and help?"

"No, you stay there. I'll bring it up. How about bacon and eggs?"

"Mmm." Mandy beamed and felt warm all over. She snuggled back in the covers and relaxed. Already this was the most wonderful day. Never had she been so spoiled. She actually fell asleep for a half-hour and was surprised when Ellie came back with the tray.

She ate steaming hot scrambled eggs and bacon and drank a cup of warm, sugary tea.

Ellie sat on the bed and watched her.

"That's what you needed. You'll be all right now."

"Oh, yes. Thank you. I really feel fine. I think I could get up, actually."

"Good. What would you like to do?"

"Well, I think I'll play in the garden for a while. What about you?"

Mandy looked at Ellie and then smiled, because Ellie was blushing.

"Oh, I know. I bet Ron's coming over."

Ellie nodded. Ron was her boyfriend. He was apprenticed to Hutchins and Company, the local cabinetmakers, and he planned to marry Ellie as soon as he had saved enough money.

"Well, don't worry about me," Mandy said generously. "There's plenty for me to do. I feel just marvelous now, so you have a nice day with Ron."

She helped Ellie carry the tray downstairs, and she dried the dishes while Ellie washed them. It was glorious outdoors. It would be lovely at the seaside. Mandy hoped that all the children were having a good time.

She went into the garden and ran to Jake's potting shed. He, too, had the day off. She went inside and carefully took down the big clipping shears. They made a sharp, slippery sound as she scissored the air.

"Oooh, I'll have to be careful with these."

Mandy hid them in the orchard and ran back to find Ellie, who was sitting in the big kitchen with Ron.

"It's so lovely. I think I'll go for a walk. Hi, Ron. Okay, Ellie?"

"Don't be too long, Mandy."

"I won't. I'll be back to check with you."

7

SHE CLIMBED over the big wall because it was quicker and there was no risk of being caught today. Clutching the big shears, she ran all the way to the cottage.

The rabbits were out playing.

"Hello, family," Mandy called out to them gently. They sat up on their hind legs, looking alert and inquisitive, resting their front paws on white furry tummies.

"Good morning, birds. Good morning, Chip."

She threw the little sparrows some crumbs of bread and put some in the palm of her hand and held it out to Chip. But he wouldn't come that close.

"All right. I can wait," Mandy smiled. She chatted as she began to work.

"Now see, I'm going to cut the lawn today, so look out for worms, Chip. There'll probably be some."

She snipped at the tall grass with the shears and the sliced green blades fell easily and quickly.

"This is super!"

She worked diligently and within an hour had it completely finished. She brushed away the loose grass and carried it to the bonfire patch. Then she began to work on the hedges. They were overgrown and thick.

Mandy hacked away at a particularly stubborn

branch and the shears went slithering all over the place.

"Oh, dash it." She sliced at the branch even harder. But the shears would not cut. The fact was that the branch was too thick and cutting with the shears was as ridiculous as trying to cut a telephone book with scissors.

Mandy threw them to the ground in disgust. "All that trouble to get the wretched things and now they don't work."

She stomped down to the stream and bathed her face in the cool, clear water. Something was disturbing her and she felt vaguely depressed. She stretched out on the mossy bank and took in deep breaths of fresh air. She stared up at the sky and noticed a beautiful hawk wheeling in slow circles overhead. He coasted on the warm air currents. She could even see the feathering on the tip of his wings. She wished she could fly, too, and be as free.

She thought about the hedge. "Now, obviously the thing to do is to cut all the easy stuff first. Then, maybe I can break the bigger branches off." She decided to try again.

Mandy snipped and cut. The thick branches stuck out and made the hedge look worse than ever.

She grabbed one with her hands and tried to twist it off but it was sharp and rough. Before she knew what was happening, she had skinned herself badly.

She began to cry. She really wasn't sure why. The hand didn't hurt that much. It was just so frustrating to have this lovely day go all wrong. It had started out so well and she had just this one chance to use the shears without Jake knowing. Now they were proving too difficult to handle. It was so frustrating.

Mandy blinked away her tears and picked up the shears once more. She was determined to make one last effort.

Angrily, she flailed at the offending branches, hacking and chopping and bending them in all directions. She got a firm grip on one branch, the shears bit into it well and she applied all her strength. Very quickly a disastrous thing happened. The shears twisted in her hands, widening the gap between the blades. The two halves were split apart by the thickness of the branch, and with a snap they broke altogether.

Mandy was aghast. She stared at the two blades in her hand, wishing that they would somehow magically come together again. The screw that held the blades had fallen into the grass. She sank to her knees to search for it. It was nowhere to be seen. Even were she able to mend the shears, they would be so out of alignment and so terribly blunt that it would be impossible to use them again.

What should she do? Should she tell Jake? Or Matron? Or just wait until the damage was discovered?

She was very anxious. If Matron found out about the shears, she must surely then find out about the cottage. At the very least, she would know that Mandy still had some secret project going. Maybe she should throw herself on Jake's mercy. She could offer to buy a new pair of shears, but that still didn't solve the problem of explaining away the accident. Telling the truth to Matron might make punishment a little less severe.

On an impulse Mandy turned and threw the broken parts as far as she could into the bushes.

The best thing was to say and do nothing at all. She would wait to see what happened.

Miserably, Mandy returned to the orphanage. She had no desire to stay at the cottage. Ron and Ellie were nowhere about. They had left a note for Mandy on the kitchen table saying that they, too, had gone for a walk and would be back soon. Mandy went to her room and pulled the curtains to shut out the light. Her hand throbbed from the skinning she had given it. She put on her pajamas and climbed into bed.

How she wished now that she had gone to the seaside. None of this awful, depressing day would have happened. By the time the children returned home, in the late evening, she had fallen into an uneasy sleep.

8

FOR TWO DAYS life went on much as usual, except that Mandy lived in a constant state of anxiety the whole time. It was almost a relief

when the inevitable summons came to visit Matron in her study.

"Mandy, Jake tells me he's missing the new garden shears, and that you were the last person he talked to about them. Do you know anything about this?"

Silence.

"Mandy?"

The bile rose in Mandy's nervous stomach. Her heart beat a loud thump-thump.

"Come along, Mandy. Let's not have any of this nonsense."

The tears came. They coursed down Mandy's cheeks. She couldn't think what to say.

"Mmm. I see you *do* know something about this." Matron looked at her and then said almost sadly, "Oh, Mandy. I just don't understand it. You've always been such a reliable girl. And now this willful stealing. It was you who took the other things, wasn't it?"

Mandy nodded.

"I thought so. Of course, you'll return the shears to Jake immediately."

Mandy shook her head. "I can't," she gulped.

"Why not?"

"They're broken," she whispered.

Another pause.

Matron seemed at a loss for words. She finally said, "I think I'm entitled to an explanation of all this, Mandy."

"I can't."

"Is that all you can say, 'I can't'? Really now, tell me what all these silly tears are for. It's so unlike you."

Mandy remained silent.

"Mandy, I must tell you that if you don't tell me what all this is about, I shall have to give you some sort of punishment. I don't want to, but I can see no alternative. Now I'm asking you just once more. Won't you please tell me what is the matter?"

Mandy was almost at a bursting point. She longed for fresh air. She was determined to say nothing. Better to take her punishment than to have her beloved cottage taken away.

"Very well," Matron spoke quietly. "First of all, you will buy another pair of shears for Jake. I don't care how long it takes to save up for them.

You will turn in your pocket money to me every week, and I will tell you when you have saved enough. Second, I am going to insist that you stay within the boundaries of the orphanage for the next week. No treats, no excursions, and early to bed."

"Oh, Matron . . ."

"Mandy! If you can't bring yourself to tell me the truth, then you'll have to suffer the consequences. Now I suggest that you go to your room and think about it. Should you change your mind and decide to tell me, you'll know where to find me. I'll be only too delighted to reduce your punishment."

Autumn

Foreboding and Punishment

1

IT RAINED ON four of the following seven days. It was the longest, most miserable week of Mandy's young life.

She had never felt so desperate or depressed. Not to see her beloved cottage. To wonder how it looked and how her precious flowers were doing. Would they survive without her care? She felt claustrophobic and imprisoned. It was terrible.

Mandy wept copiously at first. Then, as the week slowly passed, her distress became resentment, then it grew into deep anger at everyone and everything around her. Many times she contemplated leaving the orphanage and running away to the cottage. Matron Bridie would be sick with worry about her. But no one would ever find her. She would live at the cottage forever. And it would serve Matron right!

Eventually, common sense prevailed, and she resigned herself to waiting out the week. The bad weather helped a little. At least there wouldn't be much to do in the garden, and the rain would certainly help her flowers.

She spent long hours in her attic bedroom, her face pressed to the window, not caring to do much of anything except sit and stare at the gloomy, gray skies.

The worst problem was that the children knew of her punishment. They saw her anguish and sensed that something was very wrong. Solicitous and curious, they fussed and crowded around Mandy. But she gave them no explanation. Sue seemed very concerned and really tried to be helpful. That was almost the worst part of all, for then Mandy longed to break down and tell her friend everything. She ached for sympathy and understanding. But she remained silent, and that was the very thing guaranteed to change Sue's mood and make her almost antagonistic toward Mandy.

She talked *at* Mandy, rather than *to* her.

"I just felt something was going on, Mandy. I knew you'd get into trouble sooner or later."

"Let's not talk about it, Sue."

"Besides, it's not right for you to be off by yourself all the time. Everybody's noticed it."

"Oh, shut up! Just *shut up!*"

The girls avoided each other the rest of the week.

2   ❧❧❧❧❧❧❧❧❧❧❧

MANDY NEARLY wept all over again when she finally saw her beloved cottage. She was so overjoyed at being there once more. The rain had played havoc with her garden, leveling a lot of the flowers and bringing the weeds up in profusion. It was amazing that in a single week they could grow so fast.

The stream was running higher than usual because of the rain. The current was strong and the water turbulent, carrying leaves and twigs that had fallen from the trees. Autumn was beginning. The big horse-chestnut tree was bearing its fruit— rounded spiky capsules that carried the deep brown conkers that Mandy loved to collect. A pheasant picked its way slowly through the tall grass. Everything was still and gray and dripping wet. Mandy's feet got soaked.

She lit a fire in the shell room and put her shoes by the fire to dry. She was glad she had thought to store all of the wood. She made a trip to the woodpile for some extra logs.

When she opened the kitchen door, she received the most awful shock. There in the muddy earth just outside were two distinct, large footprints. Mandy couldn't believe her eyes. The footprints must have been made recently, otherwise the rain would have washed them away. They were big—probably made by a tall man's shoes or boots. It was alarming. For six months or more, she had not seen evidence of another soul. And now this.

Mandy felt scared for the very first time since she had discovered the cottage. Who could possibly have been wandering around the place? Was he a tramp? Or a burglar? Maybe he was still hiding in the woods. It was chilling to think that someone might be lurking around at this very moment.

Mandy found herself looking over her shoulder many times, as she sat before the fire. She wished she could lock the doors and close the curtains. The gray, bleak day didn't help matters either. It heightened her apprehension.

She tried to tell herself that it was silly to be frightened. Perhaps it wasn't someone bad. Perhaps it was the prince, the one she imagined lived in his castle somewhere in these same woods. Mandy brightened at this possibility.

She resolved to be more watchful and careful going to and from the cottage from now on. She would notice someone before he noticed her, that was for sure.

On her way back to the orphanage she traced the ground carefully, looking for other footprints or clues. She almost jumped out of her skin when, as if put there purposely for her to discover, she stumbled upon the clear print of a horseshoe.

So, someone had been riding to the cottage.

Mandy was excited. It couldn't have been a tramp. A tramp wouldn't ride a horse. But a prince would. So her guess was probably right. She tried to picture him. What would a prince look like? Did he ride a white horse? Maybe a shiny black one?

For many days she looked for other signs but found none. The beautiful deer, Snow, came to visit again though. He usually went to the stream, late in the day. Mandy always stopped whatever she was doing to watch him. She was convinced he saw her. Certainly he must have known she was near, must have scented one who visited the cottage so regularly. He seemed not to mind, and Mandy loved his company.

She idly wondered if the deer belonged to the prince. Did the prince feed him and stroke him and have him near always? It was comforting to feel that the animal was a presence they shared.

The autumn school term began. The weather was brisk and clear. The days grew shorter and it became dark earlier in the evenings. There wasn't much time for gardening except on the weekends.

Mandy tidied the weeds and pulled out some of the dead summer flowers. It saddened her to do so. She was parting with beloved friends.

Somehow with the coming of autumn, her previous longings and depressions seemed to return.

She was a little cheered to note the Michaelmas daisies come into bloom. Pale mauve flowers, with slender, green, upward-growing leaves. She discovered a few straggly chrysanthemums. The holly trees were showing a lot of red berries. The more berries, the harder the winter, people said.

Matron informed Mandy that she would deduct six weeks of her pocket money in order to pay for a new pair of shears. When all was said and done, Mandy felt that she had been let off lightly, considering what might have happened as a result of the incident. Though she would never forget the misery or the anxiety she felt during her week's detention, nevertheless she had still managed to keep her secret. And that was worth almost anything.

3

SUE INFORMED Mandy one day that she was going to take a walk by the gate in the stone wall. She said it somewhat defiantly. Then she looked directly at Mandy and added nonchalantly, "You can come, too, if you like."

Mandy felt she had no choice. She had been avoiding this for so long. Sue had once intimated that she thought Mandy used the gate all the time. She was sure Sue was only going there because she knew Mandy didn't want her to. Mandy anxiously wondered just how long it would be before someone inevitably discovered the cottage, as she had done. It was a depressing thought. Reluctantly, she trudged along the road, silent and angry, beside Sue.

It was a total surprise to both girls when they reached the gate to discover that it was locked. There was a brand-new chain and padlock attached to the iron bars.

Sue asked, "Did you put this on, Mandy?"

"No, I was just about to ask you." Mandy stared at it, somewhat dazed.

"Not me. I wonder who did."

Mandy was thinking of all the people who might want the gate locked. Matron? Possibly. Jake? That was more probable. He could have discovered the open gate and locked it to prevent any orphanage children from going through. It was very puzzling though. The only other thought that occurred to her was that it was somehow all connected with the footprints she had found. Perhaps that unknown someone was responsible for the padlock and chain. Her heart skipped a beat.

"Well, it looks like you won't be walking this way anymore." Sue looked slyly at Mandy.

Mandy shrugged with a couldn't-care-less attitude. "Let's go look for blackberries," she said, proud of herself for not rising to the bait.

She was glad that the gate had been locked. Maybe it would stop Sue from being so suspicious of her. But now she would have to climb the orchard wall again. And that was a problem. It was always risky.

4

NOVEMBER CAME roaring in with gusty winds
and more wet weather. Mandy's depression would
not go away. Her garden seemed sad, too. It was
virtually empty now, and the few brave flowers
that remained were flattened by the rain, their
yellow stalks sprawling in all directions. Most of
the trees were bare, and the woods had a wet
carpet of leaves.

The cottage was damp and cold. Drafts came
sharply through every crack in the walls and even
into the shell room. Mandy kept a fire going as
often as possible. Her supply of wood was not large
and would soon be finished. It was impossible to
collect more because of the rain.

She longed for the spring to come again, for
sunny days and a time when she could plant
her garden once more and watch it grow. The
prospect of the long, cold winter made her de-
spondent.

Matron informed her that she could keep her

earnings again from the Jennings' store. The shears were finally paid for.

Mandy immediately purchased more matches and a lot of candles. She often did her homework by their flickering light. In the cottage in the late afternoon, Mandy sat in an empty room, with only her books and a fire for company.

The weather remained cold. Mandy woke one Sunday morning to discover frost on the ground. She ate a hurried breakfast and slipped away to the cottage. It was becoming increasingly difficult to climb the big wall. In wet weather the bricks were slippery. She suffered scraped shins, and once she had fallen and banged her knee badly. Today her fingers ached from the cold. She paused to blow on them to warm them, but seconds later they only felt colder. Her breath hung mistily in the air. She ran to keep herself warm, but running made her chest hurt, so she slowed to a walk. She wished she had put on warmer clothes and some gloves.

When she reached the clearing she paused. The

cottage looked pretty in the pale morning light. For a moment she felt the old thrill of excitement at seeing it.

For the best part of a year she had cherished and loved this special place. It was her very own and still no one knew her secret.

There were patches of sparkling frost on the grass. It had outlined the spider webs in the garden. They shimmered and swung gently like beaded, gossamer curtains.

A sound over her head made her look up. A heron was moving in slow majesty low over the trees, its wings beating heavily at the air, its long neck extended in purposeful flight.

Mandy wondered what the heron was doing in this neighborhood. Perhaps the stream led to a river or a weir. But if it lived nearby it was strange that she had not seen it before now.

She crossed the wet clearing, opened the garden gate, and walked up the path. Suddenly she spun around in her tracks. She had never opened the gate before.

Usually it was leaning neatly alongside the fence where she had once placed it. It had been broken. Now it was mended and had a shiny new black latch.

Her heart turning somersaults, Mandy tried to remember if it had been like this the day before. She couldn't remember.

She thought of the other gate, the big iron one that had the new padlock. Strange that these two things should happen in such quick succession. Who could have mended this gate? And why?

She fetched a saucepan and filled it with clear, icy water. Then she boiled it on the trivet, and made herself tea. The hot liquid tasted good, but it hurt when she drank it down. She realized, with a small shock, that she had been experiencing a sore throat for the past two days. She really hadn't been conscious of it until now.

Holding the cup in both hands and trying to warm her fingers, she shivered slightly. She wasn't sure if it was because she was cold or if she was just frightened.

It was disturbing to feel that someone had been around the cottage again. Although mending the gate was actually a harmless thing to do, nevertheless, *someone else knew of the place* and surely knew of Mandy, too. Until Mandy found out who he was, she couldn't feel safe. She didn't like the uneasy feeling she experienced.

She didn't stay long at the cottage. Today she had a desire to return to the security of the orphanage. She couldn't get rid of the premonition that something was about to happen.

5

STRANGELY ENOUGH, something *did* happen, and almost immediately. First of all, Mandy came down with a cold. It didn't seem anything to worry about though, so she said nothing to Matron or Ellie. The last thing she wanted was to be kept indoors on account of a common cold.

The other something that happened was far more important. On her next visit to the cottage, she received the most incredible surprise. Her garden had magically been cleared of all the weeds and dead flowers. The box hedges had been trimmed and the lawn clipped. A considerable area of the clearing had been tidied, too. The Michaelmas daisies were untouched and so was the rose tree over the doorway.

Feeling already somewhat fuzzy from the cold, Mandy had the distinct impression that she was in the middle of a strange and wonderful dream. Who could possibly have done this marvelous work? Was it the same someone who had fixed the gate?

Then Mandy received the biggest surprise of all. Nailed to the doorjamb was a note—a plain piece of white paper with capital letters printed on it.

Her heart thumping, Mandy removed the paper carefully and read.

FOR THE LITTLE GIRL WHO COMES HERE. HOPE YOU LIKE THE GARDEN.

And it was signed: AN ADMIRER.

"Oh, golly," Mandy spoke out loud. Hardly knowing what she was doing, she wandered around the garden in a dazed state, touching the gate and its new latch and smoothing her hand over the short, clipped grass. She fingered the note lovingly and read it over and over again. Her excitement was so great that she wanted to shout out loud, *everything is all right now*. Whoever had written the note *must* be kind and generous and good. Not someone to frighten and hurt her. It was a tremendous relief.

But where, oh where, was the friend who had done this lovely thing? Who was he? Mandy was almost convinced now that he was her prince. Who else could have managed surprises of such magnitude?

It seemed that all her dreams were coming true. Would the prince appear one day? She prayed that she would meet him. She stayed at the cottage as late as she dared just in case he returned. When nothing happened, she slowly wandered home toward the orphanage with many a backward glance at the cottage, still hoping he would come.

What a lovely world it was. Mandy wished that there was someone with whom she could share her secret.

All night long she lay awake wondering

whether she should confide in Sue, or maybe Ellie.

As the hours lengthened, she tossed and turned and longed for sleep. But it would not come. This intense excitement was worse than any Christmas Eve, wondering what the next day would bring. Mandy wanted more than anything else in the world to solve this mystery, to meet her prince, to know him, to thank him. Perhaps tomorrow.

As the dawn crept into the sky, Mandy wearily decided, once again, that she would keep her secret to herself. When all was said and done, it was still too risky. If Matron found out, or if Sue couldn't keep the secret, the whole orphanage would know in no time.

Mandy need not have worried. By the following afternoon the issue had resolved itself.

6   ❧❧❧❧❧❧❧❧❧❧❧❧

MANDY WISHED that she didn't have to go to school the next morning. Her cold was worse.

Her head was so stuffy and she was so tired from not sleeping that she couldn't think clearly. And, of course, she wanted very much to see if there was another surprise at the cottage.

But there was a problem. If she didn't go to school, she would have to think of a reasonable excuse. If she admitted to fatigue or a cold, she would be kept at home. That would mean no trip to the cottage at all. So avoiding Matron and Ellie, she forced herself to dress, eat breakfast, and go to school. She tried to behave as though nothing were wrong.

She wondered what she would find at the cottage later that day; hopefully, an explanation of all the wonderful happenings there. Would AN ADMIRER make himself known? If he didn't, perhaps she should leave him some kind of thank-you note for his generosity? That would be the polite thing to do.

It was all so exciting. Mandy felt fevered and flushed. There was a strange throbbing in her head. It seemed that school would never come to an end. She was not interested in writing and mathematics and basic grammar today. It was impossible to concentrate.

Mandy felt tremendous relief when the school bell finally rang. At least the rest of the afternoon was her own.

She would have run to the cottage had she not been so tired. All was serenely quiet when she arrived—such a contrast from school.

Mandy looked across the clearing. Everything was as usual. Nothing changed. Nothing stirred. She experienced a feeling of disappointment. She had been so keyed-up all day, looking forward to this one moment.

She told herself that it was early yet, that she really mustn't expect too much. Perhaps AN ADMIRER was not able to come here every day.

Then, as she walked through the doorway into the cottage, she gave a cry of joy. In the middle of the living-rooom floor was an object wrapped in cellophane. It was a huge chrysanthemum plant, all russet and golden blooms, bursting with life. Nestled among the suede-soft leaves there was *another note.* So he had been here today. She hadn't been just daydreaming or letting her imagination run wild.

Mandy snatched up the note with trembling fingers and read:

FLOWERS FOR MY DARK-HAIRED
FRIEND TO PUT IN THE GARDEN
BECAUSE I TOOK SO MANY AWAY.
                    AN ADMIRER

Mandy touched her hand to her forehead. It was all so incredible. Why would anyone be so wonderfully kind? Why should this be happening to her?

She was just about to remove the cellophane from the flowers when she sensed a movement behind her. For one paralyzing moment she knew there was another presence in the room besides her own. She spun around quickly and saw a dark shape silhouetted against the light. She screamed.

Sue was standing in the doorway.

"Hey, I'm sorry. Did I frighten you?"

Mandy was speechless. For a full second she

was unable to move, but then she instinctively drew her hands behind her back to hide the note. Had Sue seen her reading it?

"I followed you from school," Sue said by way of explanation. "I could just tell you had something to do today. You couldn't concentrate for anything." She stepped into the room. "Gosh, this is really neat."

Mandy found her voice. "It's mine," she said.

"So?" Sue shrugged her shoulders. "How did you find it?"

"Oh, I—just did." Mandy felt a wave of anger. What a horrible thing for Sue to have done! How could she have followed her? What on earth was she going to say to her? How could she explain this cottage? How could she get Sue away from here?

"Is this where you've been coming every day?" Sue excitedly moved toward the shell-room door and gasped as she opened it. "Wow—look at this."

"Get out of there," Mandy said with such vehemence that Sue looked startled.

"What's the matter with you?"

"You shouldn't have followed me. You had no right to just come barging in here. That's a mean and sneaky thing . . ."

Sue interrupted, "Well, you're not supposed to be here either."

"That doesn't matter." Mandy was becoming confused. "This is my place. It's been mine for ages. Now go away, and leave me alone. Go and find some other place of your own."

She was so angry she began to cry. Then she started to cough. She felt simply awful. The worst thing was that, even should she be able to make Sue go away, she knew about the cottage now. Nothing could change that. It spoiled everything. No more secret days to herself. No longer could she pretend that this cottage was her very own place.

"There's no need to get so upset," Sue was saying. "You look awful. Are you all right?"

"Of course I am. It's just that you make me so angry. It's all your fault."

"Well, how was I to know?" Sue was getting angry, too. "Where'd you get these?" She pointed to the chrysanthemums.

145

"I bought them."

"How'd you get the money?"

"I saved it."

Mandy desperately cast about in her mind for something to distract the other girl. What if she found out about AN ADMIRER? It seemed that the whole world was beginning to collapse today. And she felt so sick! She began to cry again.

Sue looked at Mandy and then said, in a more subdued voice, "I think we should get out of here. We ought to go home. Matron doesn't know where we are. We could get into trouble."

"Don't you tell her." Mandy became almost hysterical. "You're *not* to tell her."

"All right, all right. I won't." Sue seemed anxious now and began to pull Mandy outside. "I think you're getting sick. You really look sort of queer. Let's go, Mandy. Please."

Mandy felt tremendous relief. Unwittingly, her tears had been the answer. Sue was so concerned about Mandy that her interest in the cottage was temporarily put aside. Mandy willingly let herself be led away.

"If you don't say anything," she babbled, "I'll show you the cottage another time. But you must let me do it, because I found it. Maybe I'll let you share it, too. Only you mustn't say a word."

Mandy would have promised Sue anything at this point. Better to try to make her an ally than to have her hostile and telling tales. If only she could keep Sue out of the cottage until she felt just a little better. Then she'd think of something. She wished she could get rid of the fuzzy feeling in her head.

The girls climbed the big stone wall. Mandy was trembling. She was still terribly upset and supposed it was some sort of reaction to that.

Matron worriedly accosted them the minute the girls entered the house. "Where have you two been?"

They hesitated and she looked sharply at Mandy's tear-stained face. "What's the matter, Mandy? What happened?"

Mandy opened her mouth to speak, but Sue broke in first. "She's not feeling well, Matron.

We—uh—stayed at school for a while—and then I brought her home."

Matron placed a hand on Mandy's brow.

"You're running a fever, child. Go and get into bed immediately," she said. "Sue, run and tell the cook to make a hot drink. I'll bring you some aspirin in a moment, Mandy."

7

IT WAS THE most exquisite relief to lie down in bed between the cool sheets. Mandy buried her face in the pillow and tried to sort out her chaotic emotions. Was she getting really sick? What would happen if she were? She realized that she was still clutching the note from AN ADMIRER in her hand.

She read it again. It was a great comfort. At least this was one thing Sue didn't know about.

Matron came in with a hot drink and some aspirin.

She took Mandy's temperature. "Hmmm—not

too bad, but that's a nasty cough, Mandy. You'll have to stay in bed until I say you can get up."

"Oh, but, Matron," Mandy sat up, suddenly concerned, "I can't stay in bed."

Matron feigned surprise.

"You can't?" She smiled.

"No—I—oh, please don't make me. I hate it so." Mandy couldn't find the right words. "I really don't feel too bad at all."

Matron sat down on the edge of the bed. "Well, we'll see how you go. It won't be for so very long. I've asked Dr. Matthews to stop by in the morning. He'll take a look at you." She folded her hand. "But, Mandy, I'm afraid I must ask you not to stay outdoors as much as you have been doing."

She mistook Mandy's horrified look for one of guilty surprise.

"Yes, I've been meaning to mention this. You're out all day long. We never see you. I spoke to you about it once before, if you remember. I'll say nothing more now. But I don't want it to continue."

"But why?" Mandy blurted out.

"Because it's late in the year. And too cold. I'm sure that's why you've caught this chill. Also, it gets dark so very early. I don't think it's safe."

Mandy was beside herself with grief. "No, no." She was shaking her head. "That's not fair. You don't understand. You mustn't stop me."

"Mandy," Matron's voice was firm, "I don't want any more talk about it."

"But—"

"No 'buts'—when the warmer weather comes again, we'll discuss this matter. Until then, I do *not* want you staying out until all hours. You are to return home immediately after school. And you are to stay in the orphanage vicinity on weekends. Is that understood?"

Matron's words left Mandy feeling utterly desolate. How could she explain that taking away her freedom was like taking half her life as well? Her whole being was centered around the cottage, and now that such exciting things were happening, she shouldn't be prevented from going there. But what could she say to Matron? Mandy had no desire to tell anyone about AN ADMIRER.

She was terrified that he would disappear if she so much as breathed a word.

And what of Sue? Would she say something to Matron? Or would she just investigate the cottage by herself? Matron hadn't said anything to *her* about not going out.

At bedtime Sue was quiet and concerned. She made no mention of the afternoon, and Mandy was feeling too ill and miserable to bring the subject up.

She was in a dreadfully anxious state. She tossed and turned most of the night. A wind had sprung up, and it buffeted around the big house. Mandy, restlessly, thought it a bad omen. She eventually fell into an exhausted and fitful sleep.

She never heard Sue get up and leave for school the following day. It was late when Matron Bridie bustled in to wake her up.

"Good morning, good morning." She flung wide the curtains. "Dr. Matthews is here to see you, Mandy. Do you think you can wake up?"

Mandy groggily raised herself up and blinked in the daylight. She had had bad dreams and she felt heavy-headed.

Dr. Matthews' big frame filled the doorway. "Well now, what have we here? Someone not feeling too well?"

Mandy managed a weak smile. She liked Dr. Matthews. He exuded warmth and cheerfulness wherever he went. It was always good to see him. He wore a dark jacket and faintly striped trousers. She noted that he had a diamond tiepin. He always looked as if he had just come from a wedding. He sat down beside her on the bed.

"Anything to tell me?" he asked. "What's been happening in your young life lately?" He watched her closely.

"Oh, nothing much."

Mandy wondered what he would think if she told him about the cottage. She wished she could tell him.

Dr. Matthews examined her chest and back. He looked into her throat and her nose and her ears. He smelled of antiseptic and expensive toilet water. She liked the feeling of comfort he gave her.

"Now, my dear, you're really not too bad at all. But do as Matron says and stay in bed. You'll be right as rain soon." He looked down into her

troubled face. Bending slightly he cupped his hand under her chin.

"You're *sure* there's nothing you'd like to tell me? Nothing on your mind?"

For an aching moment Mandy's eyes brimmed with tears. If she could just unburden herself to someone. She shook her head and said simply, "I don't like you to go so soon."

"Oh, Mandy, neither do I. But I have to get to the hospital. I'll look in on you this evening though. Maybe we can spend a little more time together then."

She watched him gather up his instruments and stride briskly to the door. He winked at her and went out of the room. She listened as he walked quickly down the hall and then she heard him talking quietly to Matron. She couldn't hear what they were saying.

"How is she, Doctor?"

"Well, I want her kept in bed for a few days. She does have a fever and also some faint sounds in her chest that bother me. But I'll keep a close watch on that. I'll drop by this evening."

"Anything special that we should do?"

"No. Keep her on plenty of liquids, and rest, of course. Have this prescription made up for her." He scribbled rapidly on a pad. "If she's not improved in a day or two, I'll have her brought into the hospital for some X rays." He lowered his voice. "She seems a bit sad—a little sorry for herself, perhaps?"

"Yes. I've been terribly concerned about her for some time. She has been so evasive, and I can't seem to reach her. Something is troubling her. She looks as if she didn't sleep a wink last night."

"Hm. I wonder what goes on in that head of hers! She's a sweet child." Dr. Matthews looked at his watch. "Hannah, I must dash. I'm late already."

"Thanks for stopping by, Brian."

"No trouble. See you tonight."

Mandy lay in bed staring through the skylight at the gray clouds scudding by outside. It seemed so quiet and lonely in her room now that the doctor had gone. The day stretched ahead of her interminably long.

The miserable, lonely ache was with her again. What was she to do? Dr. Matthews had said to stay in bed until she was better. But what if that were two or three days from now? Or even a whole week?

She thought of the cottage, alone and unattended for all that time. She remembered the other agonizing week when she had been unable to visit it. Her anxieties came flooding back. She sat up in bed, her chin on her knees.

What if AN ADMIRER left another note for her today? What if he returned later to discover that it hadn't been received? Supposing he gave up trying to communicate with her after a while. What would he feel when he saw that she had neglected to take care of the beautiful plant he had given her? For the rest of the morning Mandy worried the problems around in her head.

Ellie brought her in some lunch and she picked at it listlessly, not hungry at all.

If only she could somehow leave a note for AN ADMIRER. Tell him that she was not feeling well and was confined to bed. That she was forbidden to visit the cottage anymore. He would surely understand. She would leave the orphanage address on the note, too. Then one day they could arrange to meet. Perhaps in the spring.

But how was she to get the note to him? If only she could visit the cottage just once more.

She considered taking Sue into her confidence after all. But she wouldn't be back from school until the late afternoon. What if Sue didn't return from school, but went straight to the cottage to see it again for herself? It was possible that AN ADMIRER would leave a note for Mandy as he had before, and Sue would discover it.

It was these last thoughts that drove Mandy to a foolish decision. No matter how dangerous and risky the undertaking, and even should Matron find out and give her the worst possible punishment, she had to get to the cottage herself. Today!

8

MANDY PRETENDED great fatigue. She told Ellie that she thought she would sleep all afternoon and asked if she would mind leaving her alone until she woke up and called for her.

Ellie was only too delighted. She pulled up the curtains in Mandy's room and made a big fuss about tucking her in and getting her comfortably settled.

"Please close the door, Ellie, so I don't hear any noise."

"Right-ho. Sleep well, Mandy."

"Mm. Thank you."

Mandy waited a good five minutes. Her heart was thumping loudly. The big house seemed very quiet. None of the older children were home from school yet. The younger ones were either resting or attending classes.

She got out of bed as quietly as possible and pulled on some slacks and a sweater. She was nervous and her legs felt wobbly.

She stuffed a pillow into her bed and rearranged the covers over it in such a way that anyone looking from the door would think she was still huddled under the blankets, fast asleep.

She hoped no one would bother to check on

her. With any luck, she would easily be back within the hour.

Pulling open her bedroom door, she looked down the corridor. Not a soul in a sight. She stealthily made her way down the stairs. It was quite terrifying to imagine being caught and she had no ready explanation for her disobedience. She didn't dare think of the consequences if someone should see her. She paused at the bottom of the stairwell and tried to gauge where the sounds in the house were coming from. She could hear Alice in the kitchen talking to Ellie. A typewriter clacked in Matron's study. Quietly running to a side door, Mandy tentatively opened it and was greeted by a blast of cold air. It was blowing hard outside.

The wind was whipping around the corners of the big house. Ominous clouds chased each other across the gray sky.

Mandy hesitated. The cold air penetrated her clothing and seemed to reach to her very marrow, making her aware how feverish and vulnerable she was. But she had come this far and, having made the effort, it seemed silly to turn back now. It was imperative that she leave some word for AN ADMIRER. If she kept moving, she would stay warm.

She hurried through the orchard, keeping low in case someone spotted her. She came to the foot of the big wall and looked up. It towered above her head. She had not noticed how really high it was until today.

If only the big gate could have remained unlocked, she wouldn't have to make this terrible climb. Shivering, Mandy grasped for the familiar footholds and slowly pulled herself to the top. The wind sighed through the orchard. The branches of the apple tree whipped across her face.

She had just lowered herself to the ground on the other side when the deluge began. It seemed as though the heavens opened up and descended in one massive torrent. The rain poured down.

Mandy was at her wit's end. Fearful and already soaking wet, she wondered what she ought to do. She didn't have the energy to climb back over the wall. Taking refuge under a tree seemed foolish. That way she would only get colder and wetter. It was better to push on toward the cottage.

Though she had traveled the path so many hundreds of times before, the driving rain obscured everything and for a moment she was even unsure that she was going in the right direction. But then a flash of lightning split open the sky and she saw for an instant the clearing and her little cottage brilliantly illuminated in the furious downpour. She ran the last hundred yards or so and stumbled through the doorway just as the rumbling thunder crashed out directly overhead.

9 &CXRE@&CXRE@&CXRE@

MANDY WAS soaked to the skin. Her teeth were chattering. She felt horribly dizzy, and she had a sharp pain in her chest from running so hard.

Inside the cottage it seemed unusually dark. The stormy sky made it seem like night instead of midafternoon. She went to the kitchen cupboard and fumbled for the matches. She found candles and lit them. They flickered fitfully in the draft.

Was there another note from AN ADMIRER? Mandy wandered through the house looking for some sign that he had returned. She found none. Possibly he hadn't come because of the bad weather.

She was concerned about being so wet. Instinct told her that her fever was higher. The first thing to do was to get dry somehow.

She gathered the last of her firewood and managed to get it burning in the grate. She huddled close to it, her clothes steaming. But the warmth made her feel sick and she moved away. She wished there were somewhere she could lie down.

It was so cold that she tugged one of the curtains down from the window and wrapped it about her. Lightning flashed and she recoiled in fright.

She began to talk aloud in order to comfort herself. "I mustn't forget what I came here to do. I shall write my letter. That's the most important thing. Then I shall try to get home." Again the thunder rumbled overhead.

For the first time, the orphanage seemed an

awfully long way away. Mandy began to worry that she would not make it back through the woods. She felt so weak.

"What I'll do is just rest here a while, 'til I feel a little better. And the storm will go away. And then it will be easy."

She found a pencil and some paper and wondered what she should say to AN ADMIRER. It was difficult to concentrate. Her hand was shaking. She printed as best she could, DEAR SIR.

It didn't look right on the paper and she crumpled it up and tossed it on the fire. On a fresh piece she wrote:

DEAR ADMIRER

I AM NOT FEELING WELL AND
CANNOT COME TO THE COTTAGE
ANYMORE.

She hesitated, then crumpled the piece of paper up, too. What a silly thing to write! What would AN ADMIRER think of her? Just because she was sick didn't mean that she couldn't come to the cottage *ever again*. Though, in fact, that was what she was trying to say, wasn't it? Mandy wished she didn't feel so muddled.

She began again, laboriously:

DEAR FRIEND

The words seemed to blur in front of her. Mandy put a hand to her brow and was amazed to feel how burningly hot her forehead had become.

"Oh dear." She looked up and saw the flickering candlelight playing over the luminous shell walls. They seemed to be undulating waves of mother-of- pearl. The lightning flashed again, and through the window the bare trees were silhouetted agains the turbulent sky. Mandy held her breath in very real panic.

If only somebody could be with her. She wished now that she had waited for Sue before coming to the cottage. She would never have come at all if she had known there was going to be a storm like this. If only there were someone here to talk to. Even Chip, the sparrow, would have been company. The little bird was probably tucked away somewhere, safe and dry. Mandy wondered about the beautiful deer Snow. Was he alone out there trembling and frightened by the noise and the lightning? Perhaps the prince had taken Snow into the castle for warmth and shelter. She hoped so.

Mandy remembered her letter and absently picked up the pencil to write once more. Her brain seemed to be turning around and around. Why had she come? To write the letter, of course. But how silly! The prince couldn't possibly come here today. Not in this weather. What was so important about a letter? Something to do with Sue. And Matron would be so angry.

DEAR FRIEND,

I AM VERY SICK. AND I AM WORRIED THAT

A stabbing pain went through her chest, and Mandy was suddenly very short of breath. There was a loud crash against the window, and she screamed and stumbled to her feet. She had a glimpse of some wild, storm-frightened bird careening off into the darkness. She stepped back and fell against the stool that she had been sitting on. The room spun about her. Mandy whimpered in fear and pain, rocking herself backward and forward.

If only the fire hadn't burnt out. The candles were dripping, crying like the black skies outside. There were more flashes of light and the walls seemed to be coming in close to fall on top of her. *Go away.* There were dark shadows all around her. And a shape in the corner, like a man. Arms raised high.

But this is *my* house, she thought. *Get out.* Oh, please, don't frighten me so. Stop this spinning in my head. This pain in my chest. This noise. Will someone come from the orphanage? Will they know that I've gone out into the storm? But no one will know where to look for me.

Mandy's panic was suddenly so great that she managed to stumble to her feet. She had to get away from the cottage. She must somehow get home.

She flung the shell-room door wide and was greeted by a blast of icy air and sheets of rain driving in through the open front door.

The lightning split the sky once more, and it was too much for Mandy. Too frightened now and too ill to go anywhere, she sank to the floor, her hands over her ears to shut out the fury and the noise all around her.

"Mummy," she heard herself crying. "Oh, Mummy."

And then black spinning darkness engulfed her.

10

MATRON BRIDIE stared at Ellie in some consternation.

"What do you mean, she's not there?" she asked.

"Just that, ma'am. I went up to wake her like you said. But she's not in her bed."

"Well, she's probably in the bathroom. Did you look?"

"Yes, I . . . ma'am, her bed had the pillow all stuffed down, like it was meant to be her, still lying there."

There was a pause. Hannah Bridie felt a growing sense of apprehension. She had felt the same the previous evening, but she had not really examined her feelings at the time. Now, it seemed she should have been more aware. She should have watched Mandy more closely.

"What on earth is that child up to!"

She swept past Ellie and climbed the stairs to the attic bedroom. She wanted to see for herself. Mandy was obviously not there, and the bed did have a deliberately "made-up" look. The pillow lay neatly beneath the covers, looking very much like a body asleep.

"Mandy," Matron called the name once in the darkened room. She knew there would be no answer. There was just the sound of the rain pounding down on the attic roof. Slowly she made her way down the stairs again. She was very concerned.

Ellie was waiting at the foot of the stairway.

"Dr. Matthews is here," she said quietly.

Matron paused a moment and then said, "Come with me, Ellie." She walked into her study.

Dr. Matthews was standing by the fire. He was shaking drops of rain from his hair and wiping his forehead with a handkerchief.

"My God, it's a dreadful evening out there. I got soaked just coming in from the car."

"Brian, a very worrying thing has happened. It's unbelievable, but Mandy is missing. We can't find her. Ellie went to her room to wake her up just now and she wasn't there."

"What!" The doctor looked startled. "What do you mean?"

"A pillow has been left deliberately between the sheets of the bed. It looks as though she meant us to think that she is still there."

"But why would she do that? Surely she didn't go outside?"

"I've no idea. I can't see why she would on such a terrible day. Unless she was delirious or sleepwalking or something!"

"She seemed fine, Matron, when I put her down to rest," Ellie spoke up.

"But, good God, if she is out in this weather she'll catch her death." The doctor spoke on a

169

rising note of anxiety. "She could come down with pneumonia in two seconds flat. That child shouldn't be out of bed at all."

Matron turned to Ellie.

"Ellie, I want you to look all over the building. Don't say a word to anyone. Maybe she went to the kitchen to see Alice. Try there first. We mustn't panic about this until we're quite sure she's not in the house. Oh, and, Ellie, find Sue and send her to me." Ellie nodded and hurried out.

"Why Sue?" The doctor was surprised.

"Oh, just a thought. She and Mandy are very close. And something about the way they came home from school yesterday—it was when I first noticed Mandy was sick."

Matron thought back to the moment when she had seen Sue and Mandy entering the big house. Mandy had not only looked sick, but she had seemed upset and distraught as well. But the events that followed had taken Matron's mind away from that fact. She recalled it was then that she had first felt some vague apprehension.

"What if she's not in the house?" Dr. Matthews was asking.

"Then I suppose I should call the police or something. Oh, dear."

"Mmm." The doctor drew a pipe out of his pocket and lit it. "Don't worry, Hannah; she can't have gone far. There's probably some very simple explanation for all of this."

There was a knock on the door and Sue came in. Matron tried to hide her anxiety as she spoke. "Sue, here's a fine thing. The doctor is here to see Mandy, but we can't seem to find her."

Sue looked from the doctor to Matron and back again. She hesitated.

"Have you see her at all? Did you see her go anywhere?"

"No, I . . . Ellie told me not to disturb Mandy because she was sleeping. So I stayed downstairs when I got home."

"Then we have no idea how long she's been gone." Dr. Matthews looked significantly at Matron.

"Sue, this is very serious." Matron spoke slowly and clearly. "We think Mandy has run away. Or perhaps she's hiding. I don't know. But she must be found. Otherwise she could become very ill. Do you have any idea where she might be?"

"Well . . ." The young girl paused, frowning. Then she came to a decision. "She may have gone back to the little cottage in the woods."

Matron was aware that she must have had an incredulous look on her face. "What cottage in what woods?"

"The one over the wall, ma'am."

"You mean over the big orchard wall? But why would Mandy go there?"

Dr. Matthews cut in. "Isn't that part of the big estate? A man called Bill Fitzgerald just bought it."

"I think so." Matron Bridie tried to gather together her thoughts. "But, Sue, that's ridiculous. How could she get over the wall? What did she do, climb it?" Even as she asked the question, she knew the answer. Her heart sank as Sue nodded her head in affirmation.

Matron sat down in the chair by her desk. "I

think you'd better tell us all you know," she said in a weak voice.

Sue recounted the events of the previous day. She told of following Mandy to the cottage and of how Mandy had been so upset and had begged her not to say a word to anyone about the place.

Dr. Matthews was plainly puzzled as to why it was all so important. But Matron Bridie understood.

She realized now why Mandy's behavior had been so strange the past few months, why she would need to steal the cups and saucers and knives and forks. She remembered how Alice had mentioned Mandy's requests for dusters and a broom. And Jake had spoken of Mandy's one time interest in a garden project. She had wondered if it had anything to do with the incident concerning the shears. Now, she knew that it all fitted together.

She pictured Mandy, flushed and anxious, saying, "You mustn't stop me from going. You don't understand," when she had forbidden her yesterday to take any more long walks.

Those "long walks" no doubt had been to the cottage, a place that she had tried to make her very own. Matron Bridie reflected that in all her years at the orphanage she had never seen a child express her desire for a home and a family more vividly. Her heart went out to Mandy.

When Sue finished her story there was a moment's pause. Then Matron spoke quietly. "Thank you, Sue. You've been a tremendous help. And I think I understand. Now, I want you to be very grown-up and not say a word about this, about the cottage, or Mandy, or that she's missing, to anyone. Do you think you could do that? You know how upsetting it would be to the rest of the children."

Sue nodded. "Will Mandy be all right? Will you be able to find her?" she asked in a small, worried voice.

"Yes, I think so. And we'll tell you the minute we do."

Ellie knocked on the door and came in hurriedly.

"Matron, she positively not in the house. I

really looked everywhere.'" She was breathless.

"Yes, Ellie. I think we know where she is now, thanks to Sue. You'd better run along. Both of you. It's almost dinner time."

When they had gone, Matron looked across at Dr. Matthews. She sighed. "Oh, Brian, what a worry. I'll have to explain all of this later. Right now I'm very much afraid that I have to make a phone call to the police station." She reached for the phone.

"No, wait a minute." The doctor spoke quickly. "You're going about this the wrong way, Hannah. If Mandy is on the Fitzgerald property, then the person to call is Bill Fitzgerald himself. He can reach Mandy far more quickly than the police can. They'd have to get his permission to go to the cottage anyway. It would waste a lot of time. We need to reach the child as fast as we can."

Matron hesitated. "Yes. You're right. Well, at least I can try. Do you have the new number?"

"Yes, I do." The doctor took a small diary from the inner pocket of his coat. "Here we are: Fitzgerald, Cranton House. It's 42731."

As she dialed the number, Matron Bridie prayed that Mr. Fitzgerald would be able to help, and that they would find Mandy soon.

11

BILL FITZGERALD looked at his pretty wife Ann, sitting across from the dining table. He thought how nice it was to be having dinner with her in this cozy room. A fire was blazing in the grate. The silver shone in the candlelight. Samson, the butler, puttered at the sideboard, handling the warm plates and covered tureens with accustomed assurance. He was the complete opposite of his biblical namesake. Old and tall and thin as a reed, he had been with the family for many years.

Bill looked out at the rain beating against the sash windows. It was driving so hard that the park at the back of the house was completely obscured. It was dark early tonight. Good to be indoors at such a time. He was glad of the break for dinner.

All through the late afternoon he had been working in his study, poring over the financial ledgers concerning the big estate, trying to plan and shape the future and draw up a suitable budget that would keep them within their means through the difficult months ahead.

He turned to Ann. "What date does Jonathan finish school?"

"Mm, the sixteenth, I think."

"I can't wait to see his face when he sees this house."

"Ohh, he'll *love* it. As I do. It's so beautiful here." She smiled across at him.

"Happy?"

"Yes." Her eyes were warm and affectionate.

Samson came across the room carrying a silver-platter. He bent and offered it to Ann. As she helped herself to the thinly sliced meat, a telephone in the hallway began to ring.

"Dash it," Bill drew a weary hand across his eyes. "Why does everyone choose the dinner hour to phone? Sam, take it, will you? Tell whoever it is that I'll have to call back."

"Yes, sir." The old man placed the meat platter

carefully on the sideboard and went quietly out of the room.

Ann got to her feet. "Here, darling, I'll serve. No sense in all this getting cold." She placed the steaming food in front of her husband, then busied herself with her own plate.

She looked across at him. "How did you manage this afternoon? Are we going to be able to cope financially?"

Bill grimaced. "Just. It'll mean really pulling in our belts—using as much stuff as we can get from the home farm, that sort of thing. Think you can manage on a reduced allowance for a while?"

She nodded. "It's worth it."

Samson came back into the room. "Sorry, sir. It's the Matron from the orphanage on the phone. I told her you were at dinner. She apologized and said it's very important. She must speak with you, right away."

Bill made a sound of exasperation. "Wouldn't you know it. I'm sure the old dear just wants to introduce herself or make an appointment to visit or something." He got up reluctantly. "All right. I'll take it."

He strode quickly into the hall and picked up the telephone. He made his voice deliberately brisk. "This is Mr. Fitzgerald. What can I do for you, Matron?"

"Oh, I'm sorry to bother you, Mr. Fitzgerald. But something quite dreadful has happened here. I hope you can help me.

Bill noted the anxiety in the woman's voice.

"We've just discovered that one of my girls is missing. It's hard to tell how long she's been gone. The worst part is that she is quite sick. She had a fever this morning, and I can't imagine what made her get up and leave the orphanage."

"Good Lord!"

"I think she may be on your property. That's why I'm calling. I was going to call the police, but I wanted to ask you first if you could possibly help us find her."

"Is she dark-haired—about ten years old?"

"Yes." Matron sounded surprised. "One of her friends thinks she may be in an old building in the woods. You know, near the wall that divides your property from ours?"

"The Shell Cottage," Bill murmured.

"Yes—yes, that's it. Oh, do you think you could check for me? I'm really quite worried. She could be seriously ill by now."

"I'll certainly do my best. I'm glad you called. Look, I'll get onto it right away. And I'll call you back."

"Oh, thank you." There was relief in the woman's voice.

"Give me your number." Bill scribbled hastily on a pad as she gave it to him. "Right. Now if I find her, I'll bring her here. Could you call a doctor?"

"Well, Dr. Matthews is with me now. He can go immediately."

"Good. I'll get back to you as soon as I can."

Bill hung up the phone and went back into the dining room.

"Ann, a terrible thing! You know that girl I told you about, from the orphanage? Well, apparently she's at the Shell Cottage or they think she is, and she's sick and running a fever."

"You mean she's out there *now?*" Ann was instantly concerned.

"Yes, the Matron's frightfully worried. Darling, I'll need my raincoat. Quickly. I'll have to go and see if I can find her."

"Should I come with you?"

"No, I'll have to take the mare. The car would never get through."

Bill ran across the hall and down a passageway leading to the stableyard. "Brendan!" he shouted from the porch.

"Sir!" The groom appeared at the door of the tack room, looking out through the rain.

"Saddle up the mare. I've got to go to the cottage in the beech woods."

"Tonight, sir?"

" 'Fraid so. We think a child from the orphanage may be out there."

"Oh, sir. Right away, sir."

Ann hurried out on the porch with Bill's raincoat over her arm.

"I brought your hat, too, darling. You'll need it. Heavens, that poor child. I hope you find her."

Bill hunched into his coat. "So do I. I wonder

if this is ever going to stop." He looked up at the rain.

"Take care, darling." Ann's face was clouded with anxiety. "I'll turn down a bed and put some water on to boil. The child may need a hot drink or something. I'll keep your dinner warm."

"Yes. Oh, the doctor is coming on over here. He was at the orphanage when the Matron rang. *Brendan!*"

"Coming, sir."

Bill jammed his hat on his head. There was a clatter of iron hooves on the cobblestones. Brendan ran out pulling the big mare behind him. She was reluctant and nervous in the driving rain.

Bill swung up into the saddle. "Whoa there, easy, girl."

The animal skittered and slid on the wet cobbles.

"Open the gate to the back, Brendan, and get me a lantern."

"Yes, sir."

The big gates swung wide slowly. Bill eased the dancing mare toward the opening. The wind was howling around the corners of the yard. Glancing back to the house, he saw Ann standing on the porch, her face white against the darkness. She waved anxiously. He raised an arm in farewell.

The cold rain was already beginning to trickle down his neck. He turned up the collar of his coat and pulled it more tightly about him.

Brendan hurried out with a lantern. Bill leaned down to take it.

"Be careful, sir!" the groom yelled.

"Yes. Tell Mrs. Fitzgerald to turn on as many lights on the park side of the house as she can. It'll help me coming back."

"Yes, sir."

"God, what a night."

Bill bent his head to screen his eyes from the rain and urged the big mare into a canter. They went streaking out through the tall white gates and disappeared into the pitch blackness.

12

Something was making a terrible noise. It

was banging loudly and insistently, penetrating the thick fog in Mandy's head. "Get up, get up, get up, get up," it seemed to be saying. She tried to move, but, the moment she did, a wave of nausea passed over her. She lay on the floor of the cottage, retching and coughing, reaching out for something to hold on to until the world stopped spinning. She could not lift her head. It seemed the heaviest part of her body. She must be in the middle of some terrible nightmare. She would wake up soon and everything would be all right again.

"Get up, get up, get up, get up." Oh, stop the noise. Please, stop! Mandy drew her knees up close to her chest and slowly rolled over on to them. She lay in a crouching, kneeling position. Opening her eyes, she saw her hands on the floor in front of her. They looked strangely large and thick. The banging noise was coming from directly above her head. She managed to look up. A strand of the rose tree was whipping in the wind against the frame of the doorway. Sharp, cruel lashes. "Get up. Get up."

The sky outside was vividly bright for a moment

and Mandy moaned and shivered as the inevitable thunder followed. Wind and rain and noise and chills and dampness. And such a spinning in her head. Round and round went the room, then up and down, like a roller coaster, first one way, then another. And more flashing lights. One like a beacon in the dark. She shielded her eyes from the glare and saw for an instant the dashing rain and the tall trees, and the white garden gate, like a skeleton in the night.

And something else. Tall and straight—silhouetted, standing still out there. It seemed to be reaching for the sky. She closed her eyes and when she opened them again, the vision came sharply into focus. It was a knight on horseback. Mandy thought it was her prince. Had he worried about her in the storm and come to rescue her? He held a lamp high above his head and looked around in the rain as though he were lost and needed to find his way. Mandy cried out. The light swung around in her direction, and she knew that he had seen here.

The tall shape moved. Mandy could not see a face in the darkness, but as the silhouette came

closer, she saw that it wasn't a knight or her prince, but a giant, with long legs and feet so large that they swallowed up her garden in three strides. Wild-eyed and terrified, Mandy backed away. Arms reached out for her and she screamed and couldn't stop screaming. Incoherent words came tumbling out, too.

She struggled weakly, but the arms were strong and lifted her high into the air.

"It's all right, little girl. It's all right. No one's going to hurt you." But still Mandy cried out and fought against the softness that was being wrapped around her shoulders. She moaned and the world was spinning again. There was movement and motion and the voice kept on talking, softly.

Mandy was so weak and exhausted that she couldn't fight for long. Little by little she quieted and lay still, her senses spinning down, down into unconsciousness again. She whimpered and turned her face away from the driving rain. She felt rough cloth against her cheek. To her surprise it smelled good and felt warm. The arms about her were firm, holding her tight. She burrowed closer. Rocking gently in the dark night, she sensed the strong body moving with her. And still the voice spoke soothingly and continuously.

"There we are, little girl. Nearly home now. You'll be all right soon. Everything is over now. There, there, don't cry."

And though the pain in her chest and head was still terrible and she had never been as ill in her life, Mandy heard the words, and instinct told her that the nightmare was passing. The worst was behind her.

Winter

A Christmas Wish

1

THE DAYS THAT followed were distorted and terrifying for Mandy. Afterward she couldn't recall whether they had been reality or whether they were still part of her dream. She was delirious most of the time; her fever was dangerously high.

Whenever she opened her eyes she discovered she couldn't focus on anything. There was a vibrating sensation in her body. A constant buzzing in her head.

She was conscious of voices from time to time. She recognized Dr. Matthews' and thought she heard Matron Bridie's, too. But other voices were unfamiliar. She couldn't place them. And just as she tried to grasp what they might be saying to her, they would fade away or roar so loudly she thought her head would explode with the noise.

At times she felt a soft, cool hand on her brow, and saw a woman's face, sweet and concerned. And often an arm was about her shoulders and a cup of liquid held to her lips. Mandy was aware of tender and loving care, but sometimes it threatened to become the nightmare again and she cried out in fear.

When she drank to ease her parched throat, the cup in front of her often seemed as small as a thimble and her lips would feel so thick and swollen it was impossible to encompass it. Then, again, the cup would appear as large as a bowl and she would have to adjust to that.

She was incredibly weak and couldn't move without someone helping her. The effort of breathing required all the strength she possessed. As she fought for air she heard the sounds that her breathing made and felt the painful thickness in her chest.

Once, she vaguely heard Dr. Matthews' voice, serious and far away. "She mustn't be moved. She should stay here." And there was the sharp prick of a needle and always the burning skin and limbs aching from fever.

But gradually the pain lessened and her temperature subsided a little. She no longer cried out and spoke deliriously. Sleep claimed her for long, restoring periods. If she did wake in the dark and lonely nights, then the woman with the soft voice was miraculously there to soothe and comfort her.

Finally, the day came when Mandy awoke to discover that the world was no longer out of focus. She opened her eyes slowly and became aware of a soft pink room and watery sunlight shining gently through transparent curtains at a high window. Mandy slowly turned her head and saw a chair, a fireplace, a table in one corner of the room with bottles and glasses and a thermometer on it. A pretty coverlet was on her bed.

She looked up and noticed every detail of the ceiling—molded plaster flowers and garlands standing out in sharp, clear relief.

She stirred and immediately there was a movement beside her. The lady with the sweet face had been sitting in a chair near her bed. Now she came to her and smiled.

"Hello, Mandy. It's good to see you awake at last." The gentle voice was warm and friendly. "How are you feeling?"

"A bit thirsty," Mandy spoke shyly.

"Well, that's easily remedied—here." She filled a glass with water and helped Mandy sit up to drink it.

"I've been wondering when you would finally open your eyes. You know, this is the first time you've been really awake in three whole days."

"Oh." Mandy wondered where she was. And why she wasn't at the orphanage.

"You've been a very sick little girl."

"Yes." She lay back against the pillow.

Everything seemed too bright. The light from the window made her head ache. She couldn't understand why it was all so clear and sharp. Why the room and even the woman—her face, dress, the ring on her finger—stood out in such detail.

This clarity of vision was such a contrast to the confusing period she had just been through that it was almost painful. Mandy closed her eyes again. Better to shut it all out.

She heard a door open quietly. The lady spoke softly. "Oh, Bill, she's awake. She just came to and seemed quite lucid."

"Good." Mandy heard someone move toward

the bed, and she felt a hand on her brow. "Fever's gone down, too, I should say."

Mandy would like to have seen who it was who spoke. There were so many questions she wanted to ask.

But, somehow, the thought of facing the world so soon was too much. Too real, too immediate. If she could keep her eyes closed just a little longer, it was so comfortable in the bed, and everything would wait until another day. She turned away and let herself slip down into sleep again. The voices beside her faded away.

"It'll be a while yet before she's able to sit up and take notice. This was an emotional illness, too."

"Yes. Poor child. She'll need a lot of rest. And love."

2 ❧❧❧❧❧❧❧❧

MUCH LATER Mandy awoke to find Dr. Matthews standing beside her. It was dark outside the window, and a soft light was burning in one corner of the room.

"Hello." She managed a weak smile.

"Well, it's about time you woke up, young lady. How are you feeling?"

"Much better."

"You look better, too. You've been quite a sorry sight these past few days."

"What happened?"

"Ho—what didn't happen!" Dr. Matthews sat down beside her on the bed and took her hand. "Do you remember anything at all?"

Mandy tried to recall the pattern of events leading to her illness. It was too much of an effort to concentrate. She shook her head.

"Well, briefly, you were found in a cottage in the woods. You remember leaving the orphanage?"

"Yes." Memory came flooding back. Mandy's heart sank.

"A man named Mr. Fitzgerald brought you to his house, which is where you are now." The doctor spoke slowly and quietly. "You've had a nasty bout with pneumonia. We decided to keep you here because I didn't want you moved at all."

"Oh. Where's Matron?"

"At the orphanage. She'll be by tomorrow."

"Is she angry with me?"

"No, I don't think so. She's very worried about you, though. You gave her a bad time there for a while."

"Oh, dear." Mandy's fingers clutched anxiously at the coverlet.

"But it's over and done with now." The doctor's voice was firm. "The main thing is for you not to worry about anything. I want you to concentrate on getting well. Are you hungry? Could you eat something?"

Mandy was surprised to discover that she was hungry. Dr. Matthews went off to arrange for some food for her, and she lay back in her bed, looking at the pretty room and wondering how it was that she came to be here.

Compared with her room at the orphanage, this room was very large. She wondered if the rest of the house was big, too. What did it look like? Was there a garden? She tried to see out of the window, but it was too dark.

What would Matron say when she came to see her, tomorrow? Would she be annoyed? Would she insist that Mandy be returned to the orphanage? She hoped not.

There was the sound of footsteps coming toward her room, and the doctor came in again. Mandy recognized the woman with him. She carried a tray of food.

"Mandy, this is Ann Fitzgerald. This good woman has been with you night and day since you got here."

"Hello, Mandy. We spoke earlier, didn't we?"

Ann helped Mandy to sit up, and she arranged the pillows behind her back. "There, how does that look to you?" She placed the tray on Mandy's knees.

"Mmmm—fine, thank you." But she was suddenly too weak to pick up the spoon for the broth, and she lay back listlessly.

"Let me help." Ann took the bowl and gently fed Mandy spoonfuls of the warm liquid. Dr. Matthews sat close by and nodded approvingly. He kept up a stream of cheery conversation, watching her closely all the while. Mandy was glad to have him near.

"May I say hello, too?" A tall man entered the room and crossed quietly to the bedside. Mandy recognized the voice. It had been part of her dream—part of the nightmare, too.

"Mandy, this is my husband Bill," Ann said. Mandy looked up and knew this was the knight she had seen on horseback in the rain. This was the man who had brought her to safety here. She faintly remembered the horror of that time. She shuddered and managed to say, "Thank you very much for all you've done. You've been very kind."

"Oh, my dear, it's been a pleasure." He had a nice smile and laughing gray eyes. "Are you feeling better?"

Mandy nodded. For some reason she felt a little tearful. Why were they all being so good to her? She blinked and looked away.

Everyone started to speak at once.

Dr. Matthews got up and announced that it was time for her to rest again. Ann whisked away the tray and helped her lie down once more. She and her husband prepared to leave the room.

"Wait." Mandy found her voice. "Could you—could you please just tell me what happened. I mean how it happened, and why I'm here."

"Well," Bill looked quickly across to Dr. Matthews as if seeking permission to speak, "let's see now. As far as I can gather, it was like this. Matron discovered you were missing. But she had no idea where you were. Then someone called Sue, I think—is that your friend?—told her that you might be at the cottage which is on my property, you see. So Matron called me to help, and I went out on a frightful, rainy night and found you and brought you home. Does that make sense?" He smiled.

Mandy nodded. It suddenly all made sense. It was Sue who had really saved her. She alone knew that Mandy might have gone to the cottage. How fortunate it was, after all, that Sue had followed her that day and discovered the cottage for herself. But for that, Mandy might never have been found. It was a chilling thought. Her rescue seemed like a miracle.

Dr. Matthews spoke up. "Now, young lady. You may look better, but you've got a lot of convalescing to do. That's enough excitement for one night." He tucked Mandy down in bed. She was exhausted and only too glad to be lying flat on her back again.

Bill and Ann said good night and presently the good doctor departed also, promising to return the following morning.

Mandy drifted into sleep and wasn't sure if it were minutes or hours later that she felt the familiar, cool hand on her brow. The woman's soft voice whispered, "Good night, Mandy. Sleep well. I'll be here if you need me."

3 ❧❧❧❧❧❧

THE DAYS passed and Mandy improved rapidly. She looked better and felt much better. But she still had a cough that threatened to tear her insides apart.

It wasn't long before she was able to feed herself and take notice of much that was going on around her.

She met Mary, the middle-aged cleaning woman, who came every day except Sundays to help Ann with the house. And she also met Sally, the cook.

One cold, clear morning there was a knock on her bedroom door. An old, thin man entered, his arms full of wood.

"Good morning, Miss. Is it all right if I light the fire for you?"

"Oh, yes." Mandy watched him as he laboriously applied the small sticks and logs to the already crumpled newspaper in the grate.

"What is your name?"

"I'm called Samson, Miss. I'm the butler." He paused to grin at her.

Mandy laughed aloud for the first time since her illness. Such a ludicrous name for such a dear, old man. She liked him instantly.

She became enormously fond of Ann, too, and was anxious when she wasn't close by. Bill came to visit her often, and she listened for and learned to distinguish their footsteps about the house.

She was aware of the house itself now. Voices

echoed up from the downstairs rooms, suggesting high ceilings. When a door banged, it had a hollow, heavy sound, and Mandy counted the many steps it took for someone to climb the stairs.

These small details gave her the impression that the house was quite large. The impression was confirmed when she got her first glimpse of the view from her window.

A beautiful garden was immediately beneath her room, consisting mostly of low, box-hedged areas containing several hundred rose trees. Beyond the formal planting was a large green lawn leading to a wide stream which separated the lawn from several acres of pastureland. Beyond the fields were miles of woodland stretching as far as Mandy could see. It was a beautiful sight.

Mandy's bedroom was obviously in the center portion of the house, for from where she sat in bed she could see two wings of the building, one extending to her left and the other to her right. Though much larger and grander, it looked a little like the orphanage. The windows were similarly proportioned and the house was built of the same indigenous stone.

Mandy spoke to Ann about it one day. "How long have you lived here, Ann?"

"Not long at all. We moved in late this summer."

"Where did you live before that?"

"Oh, a long way away. But, you know, hundreds of years ago, Bill's ancestors built this place. Unfortunately, the whole house was destroyed by a huge fire and the family lost all of their money and had to sell the estate. Other owners restored the house over the years. It's been Bill's dream to buy it back. All his life he's wanted to live here. Just this year it became possible."

"How marvelous." Mandy was enthralled.

"Yes, it is, isn't it? I just hope and pray we can afford to keep it all going. The forestry and farming can be very productive one day, but it's a terrible expense at the moment." Ann looked out across the park. "It's means such a lot to us both. And it's such a beautiful place." Her voice was low and loving.

Mandy watched her as she spoke and knew instinctively what she must be feeling. To have waited so long to regain the house only to have the threat of losing it hanging over their heads must be enormously worrying.

Ann changed the subject. "You know, it's so cold out there today, it's just possible we'll have some snow. Before Christmas, too."

"What date is it?" Mandy had no idea.

"December, the tenth. Jonathan'll be home from school soon."

"Jonathan?"

"Our son. You'll like him a lot, Mandy. He's fourteen years old and very handsome." Ann smiled in a teasing way.

Mandy was taken aback. She hadn't realized that Bill and Ann had a child. She hadn't given it a thought, in fact. She had been so content with the spoiling and the love she had received from these two people. Now the thought of sharing it with someone else, someone much closer to them than she was, was disturbing.

She wondered what Jonathan was really like, and if he would like her.

She had the vague feeling that she wouldn't like *him* at all!

4 ❧❧❧❧❧❧❧❧❧❧

As MANDY's health improved, she received a stream of visitors. Dr. Matthews came to see her daily, of course, and Matron Bridie visited as often as her busy schedule permitted. Mandy was always a little anxious when she came. She was afraid that Matron would suggest it was time for her to return to the orphanage, and she wasn't ready to do any such thing. But Matron made no mention of it. She didn't mention the cottage or Mandy's behavior the day of the storm either. Far from being angry, she showed nothing but concern. Mandy was greatly relieved.

Alice and Ellie visited one day. Alice had baked a cake for her as a surprise. Ellie brought messages and letters from some of the children. Mandy was touched that they thought of her. But this, too, made her anxious. Any reminder of the orphanage was unpleasant at the moment. Thoughts of the past were very painful. She herself never once mentioned the cottage. It was as if it had never existed.

Sue was the most important visitor. Matron said that she had asked if she might come. Mandy, somewhat hesitantly, agreed.

Sue arrived one cold, cloudy afternoon holding a small bunch of brightly colored anemones, which she shyly handed to Mandy.

"Hello, Mandy. Are you feeling better?"

"Yes, thank you."

"Jake sent these flowers to you. They come from Mr. Simple's shop. He thought they would cheer you up and look nice in your room." Sue looked around. "It's a lovely room, isn't it? And a super house."

"I haven't really seen it yet."

"Oh, it's huge, Mandy. It takes ages to get up here. You come along this long drive. And you know that gate in the wall we found? When we went exploring? Well, it's all part of this place."

"Yes, I know."

"I suppose it was the owners who put the padlock on it."

"Yes."

"What are they like?" Sue was asking questions again. Mandy wished she wouldn't.

"Oh, they're very kind." She tried not to make her voice too abrupt.

"I met the lady. She seems nice." There was a pause. Sue looked down at the floor and then said, almost fiercely, "You are *lucky*."

Mandy was startled. "Why?"

"Oh, I don't know. Everything seems to happen to you. You're always the one who goes and does something. I never seem to have any good ideas like you do. You know, you found the cottage. And now, all of this." She indicated the house and the beautiful garden. It was a sad gesture. A little hopeless. Mandy's heart softened. She wished she could explain to Sue how often it was that she felt lost and lonely. She opened her mouth to speak. But Sue interrupted.

"Mandy, I hope you didn't mind my telling Matron about the cottage. I didn't want to. I wasn't going to tell on you or anything. But I got sort of frightened."

"Oh, Sue." Mandy spoke with all the sincerity she felt. "I'm so glad you did."

"Yes, but I know you wanted it kept a secret."

"If you hadn't told about it, I might never have been found, might I?"

"No—oh gosh." Sue looked at Mandy, her face solemn, her eyes filling with tears.

"So you see, it's really you who saved me. And I have to thank you."

Mandy felt tearful, too, and suddenly the girls were embracing each other and crying and laughing at the same time. It cleared away the awkwardness between them. They both felt better afterward. Sue sniffed and blew her nose and Mandy was so full of emotion that she coughed her hollow cough and it sounded so terrible that both girls burst out laughing again.

They had tea and some of Alice's cake and spent a pleasant afternoon together.

When it was time to go, Sue passed at the doorway. "Can I come to see you again?"

"Yes."

"When are you coming back?"

"I don't know."

"It's awfully quiet there without you. The attic seems ever so empty."

"I expect it will be soon." Mandy spoke the words

bravely, trying to be cheerful for Sue's sake. But she wished with all her heart that she need never think about going back to the orphanage again.

5

"MANDY, I WANT you to meet Jonathan." Ann spoke happily as she came into the bedroom. "Jonathan, this is Mandy."

Mandy put aside the book she had been reading. Her heart beat a little faster. "How do you do, Jonathan."

"Hi." His voice cracked with enthusiasm and ended up somewhere in his boots. Jonathan cleared his throat and took her extended hand in his somewhat moist one.

Mandy had the impression of a tall, gangling boy, his dark hair falling loosely across his forehead, with ruddy cheeks and his mother's very clear, blue eyes. He was dressed in his school uniform but was obviously restless and aching to put on more comfortable clothes.

His mother anticipated this. "You'll probably want to change, darling. But will you have some lemonade or something first?"

"I'd love it." He moved to the window and looked eagerly out across the park. His hands thrust deep in his pockets.

"Oh, Mum, this is super." He whirled on Mandy. "Don't you like it?"

Mandy had a hard time finding her voice. Never had she met anyone who exuded so much energy. He dominated the entire room. If only he weren't so tall. She was a little frightened.

"I—oh, yes—I mean—what I've *seen* of it I like." She stammered and wished she could appear calm and not so shy.

"Perhaps later on, when Mandy's able to get up, you'll show her around the house, Jon. She might enjoy it." Ann watched both children closely.

"Yes, all right." He stood nonchalantly looking at her. A couldn't-care-less attitude. "When would you like to do that?" he asked.

"Oh—I . . ."

"It won't be possible for a day or two, Jon,"

Ann spoke quickly. "Maybe, tomorrow, at the earliest."

"Okay . . ." A pause, then: "Well, see you later." A remote casual wave, and he was gone, although Mandy felt his presence still lingering in the room.

Ann smiled a secret sort of smile. She winked at Mandy and said, "I'll be back soon, darling." Then she hurried out after the boy.

Mandy was left with a distinctly stunned feeling. She wasn't sure what she had expected. But this boy, this mixture of grace and awkwardness, self-contained, yet so full of life, was certainly not what she had anticipated at all.

For the rest of the day she lay in bed, listening to every footstep that passed her door and praying that Jonathan wouldn't come back into her room. He didn't. But she could hear him about the house. The place seemed to come alive now that he was home.

She could hear Bill laughing in a downstairs room and the boy explaining something in detail and laughing about it, too. It sounded as if he were telling about some escapade at school.

At dinner time she heard the bright chatter and the clink of silver and plates coming from the dining room. It made her feel lonely and sad and left out. Later, when Ann came to sit with her for a while, she lay listlessly against the pillows, quieter than usual. Ann curled up in a chair by the fire and tucked her legs underneath her.

"It's fun having Jonathan home."

"Yes." Mandy hesitated, then bravely lied. "He seems—very nice."

"Well, you hardly got a chance to say hello to him at all." Ann smiled at Mandy, then leaned on the arm of the chair and said in a quieter voice, "He's rather bouncy, isn't he, though?"

"Oh—well—"

"I think if I were your age I'd be rather over-whelmed by him."

Mandy was surprised. Ann had touched on the very thing that she was feeling. Suddenly it became easy to talk.

"It's just that—well, I got sort of frightened. I don't know why." She laughed nervously.

"Oh, I do, Mandy. You've been waiting to see our son whom you know I adore. And you must wonder if he'll like you. Then, in he comes, full of energy. You feel you should try to like him because he belongs here. It must be very intimidating, especially after your illness. He must make you feel you could never keep up with him."

Mandy thought about it, digesting what Ann had just said. It was, indeed, the way she felt.

"Just remember one thing, Mandy." Ann looked at her fondly. "He's probably just as worried about you."

"Oh?" Mandy was astonished.

"Why, yes. He's wondering if you like him, and how he fits in here with you around. Particularly since he's been away at school." She leaned forward and stirred the dying embers of the fire with a poker.

"It will take time for you to learn to like each other. You mustn't worry if it doesn't happen. You may find you'd rather keep to yourself until you go back to the orphanage. It's not going to upset Bill or me."

Then she changed the subject.

"I wondered if you'd like to get up for a little while tomorrow. I thought maybe we could celebrate your getting better, and Jon's being home, too, and all have dinner together downstairs tomorrow evening. We could really bundle you up warmly, and Samson could light a big fire in the lounge. Just for an hour or so."

Though Mandy would rather have stayed in bed in her comfortable, safe room, she felt she couldn't hurt Ann by refusing the invitation. So she said politely, "Yes, thank you, that would be very nice." She hoped the evening wouldn't prove too much of an ordeal—with Jonathan there and everything.

6

As it turned out, the evening was a smashing success. Mandy hadn't realized how thrilling it would be to see the downstairs of the big house. There was so much to do and talk about that she hadn't a chance to feel shy. Ann insisted she take a nap in the late afternoon. She bathed and tidied herself afterward, and, when Bill came to take her downstairs, she was feeling refreshed and, secretly, rather excited. He made a tremendous fuss, taking her arm, and leading her down the big staircase with so much ceremony that Mandy felt as though she were being escorted to a very special party.

As she descended the stairway, she looked about her in awe. The main hall was tremendous—three flights of wide, shallow stairs on three sides of a stairwell. The banister beneath her hand was solid and smooth, the wood polished to a high gloss.

On the fourth side of the stairwell a tremendous tapestry was hanging. Portraits lined the other walls, each one separately lit from above and glowing in the evening dusk.

A thick carpet lay beneath Mandy's slippered feet. At the bottom of the stairs Ann and Samson were waiting for her. She smiled nervously and clung to Bill's hand. She was trembling a little, though whether from excitement or the fact that it was her first time downstairs, she couldn't tell.

Samson pushed open two huge doors, and the small party moved into the lounge. It was a beautiful room, long and narrow. A big fire was burning in the grate. There were comfortable furnishings with deep, soft cushions, and fresh flowers in vases about the room.

Jonathan sprang up out of a chair as they entered.

"Well, Jon, here's the young lady," Bill said. "We can go into dinner now. Hungry, Amanda?"

Mandy smiled at Bill's correct use of her name. "Maybe just a tiny bit," she said, trying to sound enthusiastic.

"Well, I'm starving." Jonathan led the way to another series of double doors and opened them wide. They opened on to a small dining room. There was a table set for four people. Dishes were steaming over hot plates on a long sideboard.

Beyond the table were more double doors and a smaller door set into the left wall. Jonathan explained, "That door leads to the hall again, Mandy—and look here." He pushed open the second set of double doors and stood back. Mandy gasped. She was looking into a vast, long room, obviously a larger, formal dining room. Marble pillars at either end rose to the exquisite plaster ceiling above. A huge refectory table in the center ran almost to the far wall. And the room had the same beautiful windows as the lounge.

"You know your way around already." Ann spoke to Jonathan as they seated themselves for dinner.

"I'm not surprised," Bill interrupted. "I haven't seen him all day. Have you been exploring?"

Jonathan grinned. "Yep. I found a secret passageway, too."

"Oh, where?"

"Between the second and third floors."

Bill smiled. "Oh, *that* one."

The boy's face registered total surprise.

"You mean there's another one?"

"Mm—I'm not going to tell you."

"Oh, Dad, where?"

"Wait and see."

The boy squirmed and howled in protest as his father teased him.

Ann laughed and Mandy joined in. She couldn't help it. Bill looked wickedly at them all, his eyes gleaming with merriment.

"I'll tell you tomorrow, Jon, then you can show Mandy."

"Oh, please tell us now," Mandy spoke up. She, too, was anxious to know where a secret passageway might be.

"In the back of the cupboard in our bedroom, there's a door that gives access to a passageway. It leads to another cupboard in the big guest bedroom. Long ago the lord of the manor could visit his lady without having anyone know about it. Clever, wasn't it?"

"Bill, I don't think even you know where all the nooks and crannies are in this house." Ann smiled across at him.

"I don't."

Dinner progressed. It was a joyous affair. Mandy found that she had a hundred questions to ask. She completely forgot her shyness and found herself laughing and giggling and chatting with great zest.

Ann looked lovingly at the group around the table. "It's really nice being together like this," she said.

"Here's a toast to Mandy." Bill suddenly lifted his glass. Jonathan and Ann paused to do the same. "We're glad that you're better and delighted to have you with us this evening."

"Oh, thank you." Mandy's face was rosy with happiness.

After dinner, Ann led the way through the main lounge to the library.

"Here, Mandy, you want to see another secret of the house? Look at this." She pressed a button in the molding on the wall and the entire panel slid back to reveal a small pipe organ nestled in an alcove. It was of the same wood as the library paneling—but painted with gold-leaf embellishments. Two pretty candle brackets were attached to the music stand. A small bench covered in soft, rose-colored silk straddled the pedals on the floor. ·

"How absolutely beautiful," Mandy breathed.

"This was put in the house by one of Bill's eccentric ancestors." Ann smiled across at him. "Bless the old gentleman!"

"Where are the pipes?"

"Up there, and there." Ann pointed to the wall high above the organ. "A lot of them are behind the paneling, but, see, just by the ceiling you can see the tops of them."

"Play it, Mother," Jonathan begged.

"Oh, please." Mandy couldn't wait to hear it.

"Well, some of the stops are missing, but it does still function. We'll have it restored properly one day." Ann slid onto the stool and pulled at the knobs and touched some buttons. She let her hands run over the keys. Warm, golden sounds poured forth, with the wonderful, "breathless" quality that is so characteristic of a pipe organ.

"Here, Jon, you know this one." Ann began to sing and play an old English melody. Jonathan and Bill joined in, their voices blending with hers.

Mandy listened with delight. It was a lusty, country song, and it ended with them all collapsing in laughter. Jonathan tried to reach a high note and his voice cracked dismally, quite ruining the melodic effect.

"Do you know any songs, Mandy?" Ann asked.

"Only hymns, mostly."

"Like what."

"Oh, gosh, I can't remember any right now." She was suddenly shy.

"Let's sing some carols," Jonathan suggested.

"That's right. It's nearly Christmas," Bill agreed. "Carols couldn't be more appropriate."

Ann played "Good King Wenceslaus," and "In the Bleak Midwinter," and "We Three Kings." Everyone sang loudly and, in spite of her shyness, Mandy found herself joining in. The acoustics carried her sweet, soprano voice and enhanced it. The others fell silent to listen to her. As she sang, Mandy thought that she had never been so happy in her life. And with the thought came a sadness, too. She knew she would have to return to the orphanage soon, and that this happiness would end. Her voice faded as the song finished.

Ann noticed the little girl's forlorn expression.

"That's enough for tonight," she said. "This

poor thing will collapse if we play it too much."
She touched a button and the organ rolled back
into the alcove. The panel slid into place again,
completely concealing it from view.

This procedure was enough to distract Mandy
from her own thoughts and within seconds she
had brightened.

"I think it's time for one young lady to get back
into bed." Bill swept Mandy up in his arms. "Are
you tired, Mandy?"

"No." She giggled as he held her.

"Tell you what," said Ann. "You go and get into
bed, Mandy, and I'll bring you up some hot tea
with lemon and honey. How would you like that?"

"Lovely, thank you."

"Can I have some, Mother?" Jonathan wanted
to know.

"Yes, you great lump—you may have some,
too."

And so it was. Mandy climbed into her warm,
comfortable bed. Bill and Ann sat by as she and
Jonathan drank the steaming liquid from big,
china mugs.

Later, when they had all gone and she was left

alone in the darkness, she relived every moment of the wonderful evening. It had been better than any other party could ever possibly be. She would remember it all her life. She purposely shut out all thoughts of the orphanage and her imminent return.

7

It snowed the following day. Great white flakes drifted down, creating a new world outside the big house.

Inside the house, it was warm and cozy. Ann was triumphant. "I told you it would snow soon. We're going to have a white Christmas. I just know it." She insisted that Samson light big fires in all the main rooms. Drafts from the chimneys caused the wood smoke to spiral slowly to the ceiling from time to time. It made the house smell wonderful.

By midafternoon the countryside was covered with two to three inches of virgin snow. Every tree was traced in white, and the branches of the fir trees bowed down with the weight. The banks of the stream became softly contoured. The formal garden all but disappeared. Black crows winged across the white fields, their voices cawing and harsh in the silence. It was a picture-postcard scene.

Jonathan was out all morning bundled up and ruddy-faced. He and Brendan, the groom, made a huge snowman in the stableyard. At lunchtime Jon bounced into the house, trailing snow behind him and leaving wet footprints in the main hallway. His mother reprimanded him in no uncertain terms.

Mandy slept late and remained in her room until after lunch. Then she, too, dressed warmly and was allowed downstairs. Jonathan approached her. He seemed in unusually good spirits.

"Mother says maybe you'd like to see the rest of the house."

Mandy's heart jumped. Did he really want to show her, or had Ann insisted? She couldn't tell from his expression. She hoped she need not stay with the boy for long. Seeing him in the company of his mother and father was one thing, but she knew she'd be miserably shy and nervous if she were with him alone.

Her spirits sank as Jonathan led her off down a corridor. He took her into a big, unused kitchen that in olden times had been the busiest place in the house. It had a huge fireplace and an iron pulley over it that must have held the sides of beef and pork for roasting. There were great black ovens and marble counters and wooden chopping blocks, and there was a big skylight overhead. Jonathan's voice echoed through the room. "Dad says this'll be the first room he'll restore when he can."

"Where is the kitchen that you use now?" Mandy felt lost and small.

"In the pantry. Well, it used to be the pantry. Come on, I'll show you the rest."

The boy went tearing off down the hall. Mandy breathlessly tried to keep up with him. She was too shy to ask him to slow down a little.

He took her to the top floor of the house. Here were the small rooms where the servants had once lived.

The only advantage of being up so high in the big house was the splendid view it afforded. Mandy pressed her nose to a windowpane and wondered if she could see the orphanage across the trees. But it was snowing so hard that any view was obliterated.

Jonathan showed her the secret passageway he had discovered between the second and third floors. It had a small, spiral staircase, no more than a foot and a half wide, and it was very dark. Jonathan plunged ahead, leaving Mandy to find her own way. Suddenly, in the darkness, she became very scared. Groping her way downward, step by step, she had the feeling she would never get out.

"Jonathan!" She screamed his name. She heard him running back to the foot of the stairs.

"What is it?"

"Help me, please. I'm frightened." She began to cry and stood where she was until she heard him in the darkness climbing back up to her. She felt his strong hand grasp hers.

"It's all right, Mandy. Just one more corner and there's light on the stairs. Come on now." Gently he led her safely down and she stumbled out into the hallway gasping for air.

Jonathan saw her white face and felt compassion for her.

"Are you all right?" he asked anxiously.

"Yes—I—thank you." She bravely tried to stop crying.

Jonathan looked at Mandy as if seeing her for the first time. To his surprise he became aware that she was a person with feelings and instincts and thoughts. Until now she had seemed to him to be just a silly girl who happened to be visiting for a while.

"Here, Mandy. I know what you'd like. Come and see something."

He took her downstairs, this time staying close by her side. Mandy was beginning to feel really tired but she went along.

He took her to the doorway leading to the stableyard.

"Look." Jonathan pointed outside, and she saw the snowman he had built. It was a ridiculous snowman, straw hair sticking out under a riding hat, with a whip in his hand. Already he was

229

half-covered with fresh snow. Mandy began to laugh. "He looks huffy, sort of angry."

"Well, so would you be, if you had to stand out there in the cold all the time." Jonathan smiled.

Ann came down the passageway. She called anxiously, "Mandy, come away from the door. It's much too drafty there." Her voice was sharp. "Really, Jon, you ought to know better."

Mandy was exhausted. Ann noticed the circles under her eyes and suggested she rest for a while. Mandy willingly complied and went upstairs. When Ann looked into her room seconds later she had already fallen into a deep sleep.

8

WHEN SHE awoke a couple of hours later, it was dusk. Mandy had been dreaming. She felt depressed and as tired as when she had gone to rest. She lay in bed listening to the sounds of the house. They were comforting sounds, soothing and peaceful: Ann speaking quietly to Samson;

Bill's footsteps going to his study; a door closing; music coming faintly from the radio in the kitchen. Mandy wished she were truly a part of it all.

She got up slowly and wandered to the window. It was still snowing and almost dark. An owl flew evenly across the garden and disappeared into the night.

Her thoughts turned to little Chip. She wondered if he were safe and tucked warmly away somewhere out there in the woods.

The familiar aching sadness suddenly gripped her as she gazed out at the silent world. It would be cold in the cottage. The garden would be white and desolate. There was no one to take care of it now. She shuddered. How long would it be before she was returned to the orphanage? What would she do with herself when she got back? School was probably over until after the holidays. Would she go to the cottage? Matron would surely forbid it. Did she truly want to see it again? She wasn't sure. It held so many unpleasant memories. But there had been pleasant ones, too— before the nightmare. She remembered the lovely summer and the thrill of growing her beautiful flowers and the peaceful, quiet days that were all her own.

Yet, now, as she looked back on them they seemed to have been lonely days, too. She hadn't thought so at the time. Mandy supposed it was some sort of comparison with being in Cranton House. The warmth and comfort she had received from Bill and Ann was like nothing she had ever known before. She was going to miss them desperately.

Mandy turned away from the window.

She climbed into bed again and huddled beneath the covers. Her heart was throbbing with emotion and anxiety. It was an effort not to cry.

There was a light tap on the door.

"Mandy? Are you awake?" It was Bill. He came into the room and quietly switched on her bedside light. "Ann wondered if you wanted supper downstairs or on a tray up here." He noticed her sad and tearstained face. He sat down on the bed beside her and put a hand on her brow. Mandy spoke quickly. "Oh, Bill, I think I'd rather stay up here. Do you mind?" She brushed her eyes.

"Fine. I'll tell Ann." But he made no move to go. Presently he said, "What've you been thinking about? Looks to me like you've been having a serious thought or two." His voice was light and easy.

"Not really. I was thinking about the orphanage. And last summer."

"What about last summer?"

"Oh, you know. The Shell Cottage and the garden . . ." Her voice wavered ". . . and everything."

"You did a marvelous job on the little garden, Mandy."

"Did you see it?" She was surprised.

"I certainly did." Bill smiled. "Didn't you get my notes?"

"Why . . ." Mandy's eyes opened wide. She held her breath for the longest moment. Her thoughts went tumbling and spinning in all directions. "You mean it was *you* who left . . ."

"Yes, Mandy. I'm afraid I'm the culprit. I left you the messages." Bill laughed as he saw her incredulous expression. "I left the chrysanthe-mum plant, too. Did you get that? Oh, and I had to clear the garden."

"And mend the gate," Mandy whispered.

"Yes, that as well. I've been meaning to tell you, Manders. But I wanted to wait 'til you were better."

"But how did you . . . *when* did you see me?"

"I was riding around the estate when we first moved in. I saw you working in the garden. I knew you must be from the orphanage, so I didn't disturb you. You seemed to be so . . . occupied with it all . . . and busy. I didn't want to inter-rupt. Maybe you weren't supposed to be there. Perhaps you wouldn't have come back if I had surprised you. It would have spoiled your fun."

Mandy stared at Bill. She was so stunned she hardly understood what he was saying.

Bill continued, "I got the idea of leaving you a note from time to time. I had a thought that you might like the mystery of it. It was a silly game really. I realized that almost immediately. I was going to come to visit you and explain the next time I was near the cottage. But you beat me to it. You got sick and came to visit me instead!"

Mandy shook her head in bewilderment. She was trying to put her thoughts into some sort of order. It was a painful shock to realize that there was probably no such person as the handsome prince she had imagined. He was just a fantasy. AN ADMIRER was just this ordinary human being. This kind, big, somewhat frightening man. And he had sought to amuse her with a game. She grasped for some meaning.

"But . . . what made you clear the garden? Why did you do it?"

"Mandy, I had to. There are other cottages on the estate, you know. They were all in a bad way. I needed to see what I had, so I just sent a tractor in to clear everything. Of course, I paid a bit more attention to the Shell Cottage," he smiled. Mandy felt an emotion rising within her which she couldn't understand. She had a sudden desire to weep. She turned her head away from the light and looked toward the window. The white flakes were still falling through the black night, brushing gently on the glass. Tears rolled down her cheeks on to the pillow.

"What is it, Mandy?" Bill took her hand. "Can you tell me?"

She moved her head. And the sobs shook her small frame. Bill waited.

"Won't you try to tell me?"

There was a long pause as she silently fought to gain control. And then in a small, lost voice she whispered one word, "Snow."

9

MANDY HAD a fever the following morning. Her temperature went soaring up. Though she was not nearly as ill as she had been the night of the storm, she lay in bed feeling very sick indeed.

Dr. Matthews hurried over to Cranton House earlier than usual. Ann had telephoned him the minute she discovered Mandy's condition.

He teased Mandy gently. "Now, my dear young lady, don't tell me you're getting sick again. We can't have that." After a careful examination he announced that she was suffering a small relapse. "Nothing too serious," he told Ann. "We'll just have to retrace our steps a little, that's all."

He turned to Mandy. "I'm afraid it's back to bed with you for a while, Mandy. You've just been coming along a little too fast. Recovering from these illnesses takes time." He patted her hand. "I'll come by this evening. You do as this good lady tells you, and you'll be on your feet again in no time."

Mandy felt reassured. Truthfully, she was quite glad to be confined to bed again. She was still emotionally confused from her talk with Bill the night before, and bed seemed to be the safest and most peaceful place right now. She slept a great deal, and when she wasn't sleeping, she lay listlessly, staring out of the window at the snow-covered garden.

Jonathan visited her in the late afternoon. Seeing Mandy's wan face and knowing that she was ill again seemed to scare him a little. He didn't stay with her long. Having confirmed for himself that she was still alive, he left her in Ann's capable hands and went about his business.

When Dr. Matthews returned in the evening, he brought Matron Bridie with him. Mandy had no wish to see Matron or to be reminded of the orphanage. She would be returning there soon enough. She felt petulant at what she took to be Matron's interference.

Matron requested that she be left alone with Mandy to discuss something important. Was she going to deliver the long-awaited lecture? Or was she going to say it was time to pick up the threads of her old life again?

Mandy sank down into the warmth of the bed-covers and wished she didn't have to hear anything at all. She stared fixedly ahead as Matron drew up a chair and sat beside her.

"Mandy, I have an invitation for you from the Fitzgeralds. I want to speak to you alone to find out your thoughts on the matter before I got back to them. They'd very much like to have you spend Christmas here with them at Cranton House. Do you think you might like to do that?"

Mandy couldn't believe her ears. She turned her head slowly and stared at Matron. Relief and happiness washed over her in a great wave. She was so thrilled that for a moment she couldn't think of anything to say.

Matron smiled as she looked at her joyous face. "Well, well, I see that you would like it very much indeed. I'm delighted. In that case, I'll tell Mr. and Mrs. Fitzgerald that you may stay and that I shall collect you the day after Christmas—say, around noon. How does that suit you?"

Mandy found her voice. She spoke with emotion. "Oh, that's fine, Matron. Just fine. Thank you so much. Oh golly—it's going to be *such* an exciting Christmas."

The days sped by quickly. Mandy's health improved rapidly though she stayed in bed most of the time. But she was busy, happily painting and drawing and cutting out cards as gifts for everyone in the house.

On Christmas Eve, Mandy and Jonathan made paper chains to hang in the library where the Christmas tree was going to be. And in the early evening, after dinner, Mandy was allowed downstairs to help the family with the rest of the decorations.

Bill and Brendan had brought in a huge fir tree that they had cut down on the estate. It nearly touched the ceiling. Bill stood on a ladder, and the children passed up to him the tinsel and lights and ornaments.

At the appropriate time Bill signaled for everyone to stand back and he turned off the overhead lights. Then he touched a separate switch and the Christmas tree suddenly burst into life. Glowing and twinkling in the darkened room, it shone like a fairy-tale tree. The silver and gold ornaments reflected color from the lights, and toy soldiers and gingerbread men and dancing ladies spun lazily from the branches. The tinsel angel at the very top of the tree seemed to be smiling down on everyone.

They all applauded loudly. Samson served mulled wine for the grown-ups and hot chocolate for the children, and then they all sat by the fire in the darkened room and roasted marshmallows and told Christmas stories.

Mandy felt suffused with happiness. She wondered what all the children at the orphanage were

doing and remembered her other Christmases there.

It was a surprise to discover that feeling this good was actually a painful experience. She shut out her memories and tried to concentrate on this most wonderful time.

Christmas morning was noisy and cheerful.

Mandy and Jonathan received stockings filled with all manner of goodies and nonsense and sweets and fruit. Jonathan had a toy bugle in his stocking which he insisted on blowing outside Mandy's room at a terribly early hour. He made so much noise that she laughingly hid beneath the bedcovers until he stopped.

The day swung joyously from one happy moment to another. Presents were distributed to everyone. Mandy had never received such lovely gifts. Bill and Ann gave her a beautiful red dress. It had an old-fashioned white lace collar and frilly lace cuffs and there was a pair of red shoes with silver buckles on them to go with the dress. They also gave her a tiny gold signet ring with her initials carved on it, and, miraculously, it fit her third finger perfectly. Mandy vowed to herself that she would never, ever take it off. Jonathan gave her a cuddly teddy bear made of something that was as soft as rabbit's fur. It was a dark brown bear with black ears and a black nose, and its eyes were a deep hazel color and seemed to be looking straight at Mandy. She received books to read and crayons to color with, and she thought that no other girl in the whole world could be so lucky.

At lunchtime, a light meal was served in the small dining room, and Bill told so many silly stories that Mandy and Jonathan practically slid under the table with laughter.

In the afternoon everyone slept. And later Jonathan and Bill left the ladies and went out for a walk by themselves.

In the early evening, everybody dressed up in his best clothes. Mandy wore her new red dress and shoes. When everyone was ready Ann led them all to the big, formal dining room. She flung open the double doors and everyone cried out with delight.

The room was completely illuminated by candlelight. Candles were everywhere—on the tables, on the mantelpiece, and on the small pedestal tables by the windows. It was a beautiful sight.

Bill looked at his lovely wife and murmured, "I think you must have used up this month's and next month's allowance."

Ann nodded happily. "I did, darling, but this is our first Christmas here, and I want us to remember it always."

He planted a kiss on her forehead.

"I somehow think we will."

The turkey dinner was delicious. Afterward, Ann played carols on the organ in the library and they all sang until they were hoarse.

Finally, at a very late hour the wonderful day came to an end and everyone retired to bed.

Long after Bill and Ann and Jonathan had said good night, Mandy lay in the darkness of her room, holding her new teddy bear close and reflecting how happy she had been the past few weeks. With a sudden shock she realized that it was all going to be over tomorrow. Matron was coming for her at noon, and she was going to be taken back to her old life at the orphanage. It was an unbearable thought.

Sadness overcame her, and, though Mandy fought it with all her strength, she submitted to the worst depression of her whole life.

She tried to tell herself that it was selfish to feel this way after having had such a wonderful Christmas. She was so much luckier than the other children at the orphanage. But it didn't help because, although she felt guilty, she wanted desperately for the happiness to go on. She wanted to hold on to it and keep it for always.

Mandy tried to console herself with thoughts of the beautiful gifts she had received that day. She would treasure them always. They would remind her of this best-ever Christmas. But *why* couldn't it go on? Why couldn't she stay here with Bill and Ann and Jonathan forever and ever? She remembered her conversation with Ann, and Ann telling her that they weren't sure they could afford to keep Cranton House. So, obviously, they couldn't afford to take care of one extra person as well. And even if they could, why would they want to?

It seemed to Mandy that all the good things in life had to come to an end. It had been that way with the cottage, too. She wept silent tears and her emotions spun around and around.

The night lengthened. Mandy heard the clock in the lounge chime twice. The minutes ticked away. She stared at the windows and a pinpoint of light that was the moon. And she came to a brave decision. No matter how sad she felt, she would not show her sadness to anyone. She would let Bill and Ann know that this had been the happiest time of her whole life. She would not let them see her greed and selfishness and would leave them with as good an impression of herself as possible. She would try to be strong. Having made the decision, Mandy wept all over again.

10 ❦❦❦❦❦❦

MATRON CALLED for Mandy at exactly twelve o'clock the following day. Mandy was packed and waiting for her and she kept to her resolve to be brave. It was the hardest thing she had ever tried to do. Jonathan and Bill and Ann walked outside with her to the car. Mandy felt as though she were carrying around a big floating bag of sadness inside her. It was so full that she thought it must surely burst at any moment.

Matron voiced for Mandy some of the things she wanted to say to Bill and Ann.

"Thank you so much for having her. I know it has just been the most wonderful time. Hasn't it, Mandy?"

Mandy nodded. She forced her eyes wide apart so that the tears would not show. The strain was nearly unbearable, and her throat was aching horribly. She gave Ann a brief, fierce hug and managed to whisper, "Thank you for everything." She stared at the ground as she offered Jonathan her hand.

" 'Bye, Jonathan."

" 'Bye, Mandy. Hope to see you soon."

Bill looked lovingly at the girl standing in front of him in such obvious emotional pain. He placed his hands on her head and pulled her close to his side.

Mandy buried her face in his coat. They stood that way for a long moment.

"Come again soon, Mandy. Come and visit us often. We shall miss you a lot."

Mandy could only nod her head. She tried to summon a smile and gave a small hiccup of emotion. Bill quietly handed her his handkerchief and then moved to open the car door.

"Take care of her, Matron. She's very special to us."

Matron climbed into the car and Mandy followed. Her eyes were so full of tears that she could barely see. The car door slammed and the Fitzgerald family shouted their good-byes. The limousine pulled away from the house, its tires crunching noisily on the ground.

Mandy did not look back. She sat stiffly on the edge of her seat and averted her head so that Matron could not see her. She gazed sadly out of the window.

Matron was saying, "The children are terribly excited about your coming home, Mandy. You've no idea how much you were missed at Christmas."

The car stopped at two big gates leading on to

the main road. Mandy watched the gates swing wide to let the car through, and she felt a surge of bitter resentment toward Matron for taking her back to the orphanage. She felt as though she were a piece of baggage being shifted from one place to another. She had a sudden desire to jump out of the car and run far away from everyone.

How wonderful it would be to live her own life, to be free to decide things for herself.

The orphanage seemed smaller than Mandy remembered. It looked bleak and gray as they arrived. The only cheerful thing about it was the welcome of the children who came rushing out, as the car pulled up to the front door. She was glad of the distraction. It momentarily took her mind away from the unhappiness she felt.

Mandy discovered that she was something of a celebrity. The children wanted to know every detail of her Christmas and her illness and her being away for so long. The attention was very flattering, but Mandy had no wish to talk about anything. She was achingly tired and there were dark shadows under her eyes. She found herself yawning, and Matron suggested that she go up-stairs for an afternoon rest.

Sue carried Mandy's case up to the attic, and she chattered happily as Mandy undressed for bed.

"I'm so glad you're back, Mandy. It was terribly quiet here without you. Christmas was really lovely."

Mandy gazed around the familiar attic room. It was so different from the large, airy bedroom she had occupied at Cranton House. She wished she could be in that quiet, peaceful room at this very moment. She took from her case the brown teddy bear that Jonathan had given her and climbed into bed.

"I've got masses to tell you," Sue said. "Will you show me your Christmas presents when you get up?"

Mandy smiled and nodded wearily. She touched the signet ring on her finger and gazed at it lovingly. A deep sadness overcame her and she pulled the bear close and held it tightly. She cuddled down beneath the covers, pulling the sheet up over her head. Sue, sensing Mandy's mood, wisely left the room and pulled the door to a close behind her.

11 ❦❦❦❦❦❦

MATRON PEEPED in just as Mandy was waking up the next morning. When she saw that Mandy was stirring, she came into the room.

"Good morning, Mandy. How do you feel today?"

For a moment Mandy couldn't remember where she was and then she realized that she was back at the orphanage. She sat up in bed and rubbed her eyes.

"Goodness, is it morning?" she said. Matron pulled open the curtains and came to sit on the edge of her bed.

"It is. And it's ten o'clock, believe it or not. Sue has been up and about for ages and is waiting for you to come downstairs."

Mandy thought about Bill and Ann and tried to imagine how she would get through the day without seeing them. Her insides ached from missing them so. Would she ever feel better? Would her sadness ever go away?

Matron noticed that Mandy's eyes were swollen from so much crying, and she saw the tears that threatened to gather there again.

"Mandy, Mr. and Mrs. Fitzgerald telephoned early this morning to find out how you were."

"Oh, did they?" Mandy felt a warm feeling spreading through her. "What did they say?"

"They were most anxious about you. They were glad to know that you were still sleeping. They sent their love and wanted you to call them later if you felt like it. Otherwise, they said they'd phone again tonight."

Mandy thought about this and wondered if she should return their call. One part of her wanted to most desperately. But, on the other hand, she was reluctant to get in touch with the Fitzgeralds. It would make her feel so sad to speak with them again. She was sure she would cry, and Mandy was beginning to be angry at the chaotic emotions that seemed to turn her inside out and upside down.

"I—I don't think I'll call them just yet," she said, evasively. "I mean, I've only just come back, and I want to see everybody and catch up on things, you know."

Matron seemed to understand and she changed the subject.

"Mandy, I don't want you to be too active today. Dr. Matthews told me that you must get plenty of rest. You may get up and play for a while, but just don't overdo it." She leaned forward and gently brushed aside the hair on Mandy's forehead. "Everything will seem all right again in time, you'll see."

Mandy smiled bravely. Matron was kind. She told herself that soon she would feel glad to be back with her friends again. In the meantime, she would find an excuse to avoid speaking to the Fitzgeralds when they called. It would be so much easier that way. She lay back on her pillows and prepared to face the long day ahead.

Later in the week Matron Bridie rang the Fitzgeralds at Cranton House. Ann picked up the receiver and spoke with some relief as she heard Matron's voice.

"Oh, Mrs. Bridie, we've been trying to talk to Mandy for the last couple of days. But we don't seem able to reach her."

"I know; that's why I'm calling." Matron sounded a little troubled. "She's deliberately avoiding getting in touch with you. I really believe it's so painful for her that she just can't face it."

"Oh, dear, that's so sad." Ann's voice echoed her feelings. "We miss her most terribly."

"Yes, and I know she misses you, too. She's really having a bad time of it," Matron said. "She doesn't seem to have an interest in anything right now. She is very controlled. I almost wish she would break down. I think it would help her. She was questioning me the other day about her parents and how they died. That's something she hasn't done for a long time. I think she's quite desperate to create the feeling of a family about her."

"How can we help?" Ann asked. "Should we come to visit her?"

"I don't think there is anything you can do at the moment," Matron replied, "except to keep trying to telephone Mandy. Even if she doesn't speak to you, it's important that she knows that you care. And she will settle down after a while."

Ann related her conversation with Matron to Bill. He looked thoughtfully into the fire. It was a long time before he spoke. "It's too bad. It really is. Dammit—I miss that little girl."

Ann sat down beside him and he put an arm around her shoulders.

"Well, at least she had a wonderful Christmas, darling," Ann said, trying to sound more cheerful than she felt. "That'll be something good for her to remember always." She didn't sound very convinced.

"I'm not sure if she isn't in more trouble because of her Christmas here," Bill said. "Before she came to stay with us she knew nothing of our kind of warmth and love, and therefore she had no reason to miss it. But now . . ." He didn't complete the sentence, but Ann knew what he meant. She felt miserable. She wished there were a way of letting Mandy know how badly they missed her.

12 ❧❧❧❧❧❧

AT THE ORPHANAGE the New Year was ushered in quietly and with little ceremony. The children settled down after the festivities of Christmas and prepared themselves for the new school term ahead. Routines were established once more and things reverted to normal.

For Mandy, nothing was the same and it never would be again. She could not stop thinking, painful as it was, about Bill and Ann and Jonathan. She found herself reliving every moment of the time that she had spent with them. She wondered how they were and what they were all doing. Did Samson miss her? Had Jonathan found the other secret passageway? Had his snowman melted? She pictured the family getting up in the morning. And sitting down to dinner at night. Mandy couldn't know it, but, for the first time in her life, she was feeling homesick.

The knowledge that she could not go back to the Fitzgeralds was so painful that it was almost unbearable. Mandy knew that she would certainly be allowed to visit them once in a while. At one time she would have welcomed the possibility. But now she was not prepared to settle for anything less than she had already experienced. If Bill and Ann could not take care of her and be her family, then she would go and find someone who could.

Mandy was so miserable that she made a characteristic move. It wasn't in her nature to tolerate sadness, and so she became determined to do something to rid herself of her unhappiness. Somehow, somewhere she would find a way to show someone that she was worthy of love. But she would not find it by staying at the orphanage. Matron and Ellie and Jake and Sue were all good to her and very considerate. But they could not give her the kind of love that she craved. And besides, Mandy felt that she had had enough of people telling her how to conduct her life. "Mandy, do this. Mandy, do that. Mandy, get to bed early. Mandy, don't go outside. Mandy, do as you're told."

Well, Mandy would show them all that she didn't need anyone, anymore.

She made a decision born of great desperation. She spoke to Sue about it.

"Sue, if you promise not to tell anyone, I'll let you in on a secret. I'm going to run away."

"Oooh, Mandy." Sue was immediately concerned. "Where will you go?"

"I don't know yet. But I just have to leave. I can't stay here anymore."

"But why not? It's not such a bad place and everybody likes you."

"I can't explain it, Sue. It's just something I feel inside. I can't spend the rest of my life here in the orphanage. I want to be somebody and prove I can do something. I'll probably go to a big town. I'd like to go miles and miles away," she said wistfully.

"But what will you do for money?" Sue was concerned with the practical side of things.

"I have a little that I've saved. And I'll probably find a job."

"When will you go?"

"I thought I'd try tomorrow morning—before anybody's up. I'll pack this evening and get a good night's sleep. But you're not to say anything, Sue. Do you promise?"

Sue was solemn and quiet for a moment. And then she nodded her head. "I'll help you pack," she said.

Later in the day, Sue came to Mandy, clutching a paper bag in her hand.

"Mandy, I want you to take this. It's some money that I was given for Christmas. It might help you a tiny bit. No, I really want you to have it," she said, as Mandy started to protest.

She helped Mandy put her few precious possessions into a suitcase. Mandy packed her new red dress and shoes and her teddy bear and some trousers and sweaters and two pairs of pajamas. Then she pushed the case under her bed so that it would not be seen.

"Oh, Mandy, I do wish you wouldn't do this." Sue was becoming increasingly anxious. "I understand how badly you feel, I really do. But what'll I do when you're gone? Do you suppose I should come with you?"

Mandy thought how good it would be to have Sue's company when she traveled. Truthfully, she was quite nervous about going. But she shook her head and said, "No, this is something I've got to do myself. Besides, I'll need you to cover for me as long as possible after I'm gone."

"Will I ever see you again? Will you write to me or anything?" Sue was tearful.

"Well, I couldn't write to you, silly, because everybody would know where I was. But we'll see each other one day, I promise."

The girls prepared for bed. They were both on edge and talked to each other in whispers long after the lights were out.

Mandy looked up at the skylight over her head. It was a cloudy night and she could see no stars. She hoped that the weather would be fine by the morning. She was anxious about waking up early enough. Mandy decided that she would just cat-nap all night and not really go to sleep after all.

Her mind drifted to thoughts of Shell Cottage. She hadn't thought about it for a long time. It was a pity that everyone knew of the place, because it would have been a perfect spot to hide for a while. But she wasn't sure that she ever wanted to see it again. Anyway, it was up to Bill and Ann to take care of it now.

Mandy felt sad. Tomorrow would be the last time she would see the orphanage. Maybe when she was much older she would come back to visit everyone. She wondered how she would feel without Matron and Ellie and all the friends she knew.

She thought of Bill and Ann and wondered if they'd be anxious about her after she'd gone. Perhaps she should go and say good-bye to them? It would be wonderful to see them just once more. But they would try to dissuade her from running away. And she was determined to go. There was no point in saying good-bye to anyone, except Sue.

In spite of her resolve to stay awake, Mandy drifted into a light sleep.

"Mandy—Mandy, wake up."

A voice was calling to her as if from a great distance.

Mandy cried out in her sleep and stirred.

"Mandy."

She awoke with a start and became aware that

Sue was standing beside her bed and shaking her vigorously.

"Mandy, oh, Mandy, please wake up. You'll never guess what's happened."

"What? What is it?" Mandy sat up anxiously. Sue seemed very excited.

"I heard a car coming up the drive so I got out of bed to look. No one ever comes to visit at this hour. But, Mandy, I think it's Mr. and Mrs. Fitzgerald. I'm sure it's their car down there."

Mandy was out of bed so fast that for a moment she felt quite dizzy. She ran to the window and peered out into the darkness. She could see the shape of a car parked in the driveway below, but it was so dark that she could not tell if it belonged to Bill and Ann or not. She discovered that her heart was thumping loudly. Grabbing her dressing gown she ran to the door of her room and opened it.

"Come on," she whispered.

Sue eagerly followed her, and the girls tiptoed to the top of the main stairway. The house was very dark except for a small light in the hall. Mandy crept farther down the stairs and leaned over the banister. She could see a beam of light

263

coming from under the door in Matron's study. And she could hear voices, soft and indistinct.

"Can you hear what they're saying?" Sue asked.

"No, I can't."

"Do you suppose it's them?"

"Sshh." Mandy was trembling.

Suddenly, before the girls could run away, the study door was flung wide open and Matron came out. She turned on the main hall light, and both girls were left standing in the bright glare.

Matron blinked in surprise at the sight of them both. Then, instead of being angry, she gave a slight smile and said in a very ordinary voice, "Oh, Mandy, I'm glad you're up. I was just coming to wake you. There's someone down here to see you." As she spoke a figure came to the door of the study and gazed up at her.

"Good evening, Manders," said Bill.

Mandy's heart did a huge somersault. Ann came to the door and stood beside him.

"Hello, darling," she said. Both the Fitzgeralds were smiling.

Mandy had such an urgent desire to run to them

that she thought she would fall and tumble down the stairs in her excitement. But she contained herself and stayed where she was.

"Hello," she said and was surprised at how flat and noncommittal her voice sounded.

What were the Fitzgeralds doing here at this time of night? Had they come because she hadn't telephoned them? Were they angry with her? Were they hurt?

"Well, Mandy, aren't you coming down?" Matron moved to the staircase. "Why don't you come and visit for a while, and I'll take Sue back to her room and keep her company."

Mandy walked slowly down the stairs gripping the banister tightly, feeling that her legs would buckle beneath her unless she did.

"How have you been, Mandy?" Bill asked warmly as she reached the bottom step.

"Oh, fine." Again, her voice sounded remote and disinterested. The three of them moved into the study.

"Mandy, you can't imagine how badly we've missed you," Ann was saying.

Mandy looked at Bill and Ann and a pain began in her tummy. She was so desperately glad to see them both. She sat down in a chair by the fire and folded her hands together tightly in an effort to stop them from trembling.

"Has everything been all right since you've been back?" Ann asked. Mandy nodded.

"Did you miss us?" Bill smiled his teasing smile.

Mandy wondered how she could ever explain just how much she had ached to see them both. It was more than words could describe.

"Yes, I did," she said in a small voice, thinking, "What is the matter with me? Why am I behaving so strangely?"

Bill sat down and leaned toward her. "Manders, we came especially to see you tonight because we have something to tell you. It's very important and it concerns us all. Listen carefully now and try to let me finish before you speak." His voice was serious, and he glanced at Ann before he continued. "Ann was right just now, Mandy. After you left us, we discovered that we missed you terribly. It just wasn't the same in the house without you. Even poor old Jonathan seems lost and out of sorts. We discussed our feelings and since we all felt the same way, we decided that we would ask Matron if it would be possible for you to come and live with us." Mandy's eyes widened and she drew in a deep breath.

"We wanted to come and speak to you about it right away," Bill went on, "but first of all it was necessary to find out from the authorities whether they would let us adopt you. It didn't seem right to talk to you about it until we were sure. And, of course, the authorities took forever to find your records and check your history and so on. But, darling, just tonight, we finally got permission to come and speak to you. And that's why we're here. We were so excited, we couldn't wait until the morning, so we came over right away."

Mandy discovered that the palms of her hands were wringing wet. She blinked hard and looked at the clock on the mantelpiece in an effort to control her chaotic emotions. One remote part of her noticed that the hands of the clock were made of golden filigree and that the time was ten minutes to eleven.

Ann moved forward and spoke in a warm and loving voice. "Darling, we do love you very much. We've always wanted to have a little girl and somehow you seemed so special to us from the very first night you came to the house. You don't have to make up your mind about this just yet. There's no hurry for an answer. But, do you think you could consider coming to live with us for always? I think we could make you very happy. How do you feel about taking us on as a family?"

There was a moment of silence. The only sound in the little study was the loud ticking of the clock.

Mandy found that she was completely and utterly speechless. For a moment she wondered if she were in the middle of some terrible, yet wonderful, dream. It was hard to believe what she had just heard. But one look at Bill and Ann and the concerned expectation on their faces told her that this was a very real moment indeed.

Then why was she feeling so bewildered? Why couldn't she answer as her heart dictated? Why couldn't she say that this was the most fabulous, wonderful, marvelous thing that had ever happened to her in her whole life?

To be adopted. To live in Cranton House forever. To be with this family that she had come to adore so much. Not to have to live at the orphanage for the rest of her life, or run away as she had planned to do. To know that Bill and Ann really cared enough after all.

"We love you very much, Mandy." "We think we could make you very happy." "We've always wanted a little girl!"

Suddenly, Mandy was filled with the most enormous, brimming happiness. The delayed emotion surged up within her, reaching from her toes to the top of her head, and she experienced a wildly joyous feeling of release.

She rose unsteadily to her feet and looked first at Bill and then at Ann. "Oh, gosh," was all she could say. "Oh, *gosh.*"

Bill began to laugh. Ann held out her arms and Mandy went into them and clung tightly. She had never been so happy in her whole life and she could not stop weeping. Ann bent to kiss the dark head and found herself weeping, too.

13 ❦❦❦❦❦❦❦❦❦

THINGS SEEMED to happen very fast after that. Matron came downstairs and was delighted to learn that everything had turned out so well. The Fitzgeralds were anxious to take Mandy back to Cranton House with them that very evening. But, strangely, Mandy decided she would prefer to wait until the following day. She couldn't help thinking of Sue, and she knew that she could not say good-bye to her friend so abruptly and leave her to spend the rest of the night alone.

So it was decided that Bill would call for Mandy in the morning.

The Fitzgeralds bid her a fond goodnight, and afterward Mandy broke the wonderful news to her friend. As she had anticipated, it was a difficult and ambivalent moment for Sue.

"Oh, Mandy, you are lucky. What a fabulous thing to happen. I know you'll be very happy." There was a pause and then quite suddenly Sue burst into tears. Mandy put her arms around her.

"Oh, Sue, don't cry. Please don't. Think how

super it's going to be. We'll be able to see lots and lots of each other. You can come to the house and play and maybe spend the night sometimes."

Sue nodded and rubbed her eyes. "I'm really terribly thrilled. It's just that I'll miss you so badly." She blew her nose hard.

"I'll miss you too." The girls clung to each other for a moment. Sue looked up and said. "Golly, how lucky it was that they came to see you to-night. You'd have been gone by tomorrow."

Mandy nodded. It was a sobering thought.

The following morning Mandy was consumed with anxiety. She could hardly wait for Bill to come and pick her up, and she had the terrible fear that he might forget all about it or change his mind completely. Her packing was done in no time at all since she had been prepared to leave the night before anyway. The entire or-phanage knew about her departure, and when Bill finally drove up in his station wagon it seemed that every child was waiting to say good-bye.

It was almost more than Mandy could bear. She clambered into the front seat of the automobile and rolled down the window to wave to everyone.

Matron was smiling happily and waving. Sue was smiling also, but her eyes were filled with tears.

Mandy's last impression as the car pulled away was of the young, eager faces of the orphanage children and their voices raised high in farewell.

"Good-bye Mandy." "See you soon." "God bless, Mandy." "Please come back and visit."

Mandy waved until the orphanage was completely out of sight. When she turned back in her seat she discovered that she was crying.

Bill looked across at her and smiled fondly.

"A little sad?" he asked.

"Yes."

"And happy, too?"

"Oh, yes."

"A bit of both. Well, that's understandable."

"It's silly, but I wish they could all come, too, It's terrible somehow to leave them behind."

Bill nodded. "I know, Mandy. I know. But

those children will find a life for themselves one day, just as you have. You'll see. It may not be right away, perhaps it will be when they grow up or when they marry. But it will happen. And in the meantime, Matron isn't going to let them be unhappy, now is she?"

"No." Mandy wiped her eyes. There was silence for a moment. The car sped through the country lanes and Mandy looked out of the windows at the crisp winter morning. Traces of snow were everywhere. Clear sunshine bathed the countryside in a silvery light, like a watercolor. Mandy shook her head in bewilderment.

"I just don't understand why it was *me* that got to be so lucky," she said.

"Oh, gosh, Mandy. What shall I tell you?" Bill looked thoughtful. "I suppose luck does have something to do with it. But you're a very special little girl. And I think you're strong and not afraid to go looking for your life. You know, I think you could be a good example to the orphanage children. Perhaps, one day when you're truly settled in with us and you know that we're not ever going to let you go, you might consider going back to visit them from time to time. I'm sure it would help them."

Mandy thought about it.

"I'd like that," she said simply.

14

BILL BRAKED the car to a halt just outside the big gates to Cranton House. Mandy remembered passing through them a couple of weeks earlier and how unhappy she had been. The long driveway stretched ahead. Mandy drew in a deep breath of the clear, fresh air coming in through the open window. She looked at the trees and the fields all around her and experienced a feeling she had never felt before. It was a warm contentment, something like the feeling one gets when hot tea and honey slide way down into one's stomach, only ten times better.

Bill said, "You've never really seen Cranton,

have you, Mandy? C'mon. We've got time. I'll give you a quick guided tour."

He drove the car around the beautiful estate, pointing out the various places of interest.

"There's the dairy, Mandy, and the courtyard beyond used to be the old kennels."

There were hay barns, and places for grain storage and silage and tractors and equipment. Mandy saw cows in the cowshed and a huge bull in an outside stall. There were chickens and cockerels, pigs and horses. A large, silly dog ran around in happy circles trying to scare the fowl. There was a big kitchen garden and beyond were rows of empty wire pens.

"Those are for the baby pheasants when they're strong enough," Bill explained. "We'll be breeding them early in the year. You'll see."

Bill swung the wagon onto a wide rutted track. A ribbon of water ran under a small humpbacked bridge and beyond was the flat, smooth surface of a beautiful lake.

Bill stopped the car on the bridge and pointed.

"Mandy, see the trees on the island in the middle of the lake? Notice the ragged collection of twigs and mud and old leaves in the tops of them? They're herons' nests. We must have had at least three pairs this year. I bet they'll be back in the spring."

Mandy remembered the heron she had seen flying over the cottage one day. It must have been heading for the lake. She was struck by a thought.

"Bill, I suppose the little stream by the cottage runs into the lake, doesn't it?"

"Yes, darling, it does."

"Who used to live in Shell Cottage?" Mandy wanted to know.

"Well, at first, no one did, believe it or not. In the old days it was a sort of playhouse. My ancestors would have picnics there; it was a place to ride to, to shelter in when it rained, that sort of thing. That's why the shell room was built— it was purely a fun house."

"But then . . . ?"

"Then, of course, when times became difficult and the family was so hard up, it was rented out to whoever could afford it." Bill turned to Mandy. "Incidentally, Manders, what would you like to do with the cottage? It's yours now, you know. I thought I'd make a sign to that effect and put it on the gate. And I can paint it up a bit. Would you like to plant the garden again this year?"

Mandy thought about it. She became suddenly serious. She remembered last summer and her passionate concern for the garden and the house. But, now, it didn't seem so important. Her new life promised such a wonderful future. Would she want to spend time at the cottage? She looked at Bill. And suddenly, she knew what it was she wanted to say.

"Bill, if I could do anything with Shell Cottage—if it's at all possible, that is—what I'd really like to do is to let the other children at the orphanage have it."

Bill looked surprised, but Mandy warmed to her subject.

"You know, like Sue and everybody. They could come to it and play and have a part of the garden to make pretty. I think it would be marvelous to have a special place like that. It would mean having something of their very own, don't you see?"

There was a pause. Bill's eyes narrowed in

thought. Mandy waited for him to speak. He did so finally, quietly and deliberately.

"I think it's a wonderful idea, Manders." His voice was low with emotion. "It would be simple to grant a right-of-way through the woods. We'd have to build a gate in the big wall. But it could be, indeed, a playhouse for the children." He turned and smiled. "Just as it used to be. That's a good thought, Manders. I'll speak to Matron about it this evening."

He turned the ignition key in the car and started it up again. "Now, darling, we'd better get back to the house. Ann'll be wondering what happened to us. I told her we'd be there for lunch."

Mandy felt a thrill as Cranton House came into view. The station wagon drove around a circular lawn and came to a stop in front of the big house. Bill paused a moment, his hands resting on the wheel. He grinned at Mandy.

"Well, Manders, here you are. You're home."

Mandy's feelings soared with happiness, and laughter bubbled up inside her. She gave Bill a brief hug and then stepped out of the car and raced up the steps to the front door where Jonathan and Ann were waiting for her.

"Hello." Mandy's voice was breathless with excitement.

"Hello, Mandy. Welcome." Ann folded her in her arms. Jonathan was grinning good-naturedly and he patted her on the back in an embarrassed sort of way.

Bill ran up the steps to join them and as the family turned and walked through the front door, Mandy experienced a great warm feeling of contentment. She realized that never again would she go through long nights of aching sadness. There would be no more depressions that she couldn't understand. At last she had a home and a family and people to love and be loved by.

She had found what she had been looking for all her life.